"Anna Schulz," Brian said as soon as I let him in. Then he watched my face for a reaction.

I opened my eyes wide and stared at him.

"Are you acquainted with her?" he said.

"Yes," I said. "She was Phillip's secretary. Why? What do you know about her?"

"Not much," Brian said, "except that she was found murdered this morning in Phillip Barry's office. And she had a note in her pocket with your name and phone number on it."

"Brian, I was supposed to have breakfast with her this morning, but she never showed up. She said she really wanted to talk to me but she didn't want to do it on the phone."

"Did she say what it was about?"

"No, but I assumed it was about Phillip's death. She sounded like it was really important."

"Where and when?" Brian said.

"Oh. At the Omega Restaurant on Twenty-seventh Street, at nine o'clock. At first she wanted to meet at seven, but then she called back and changed it to nine because she had to do something first."

"Did she say what?"

"No, but she said it was very important."

—————————————— ★ ——————————————

"...full of suspense and intrigue.... There are even a few unique surprises along the way."
—*Rendezvous*

Forthcoming from Worldwide Mystery by
KATHLEEN ANNE BARRETT

MILWAUKEE AUTUMNS CAN BE LETHAL

Milwaukee Summers Can Be DEADLY

Kathleen Anne Barrett

WORLDWIDE®

TORONTO • NEW YORK • LONDON
AMSTERDAM • PARIS • SYDNEY • HAMBURG
STOCKHOLM • ATHENS • TOKYO • MILAN
MADRID • WARSAW • BUDAPEST • AUCKLAND

To my husband, William E. Hoese

MILWAUKEE SUMMERS CAN BE DEADLY

A Worldwide Mystery/August 2001

First published by Thomas Bouregy & Company, Inc.

ISBN 0-373-26393-7

Printed in U.S.A.

I would like to acknowledge and thank my mother-in-law, Joan L. Joyce, for her very generous and invaluable services during my book-signing appearances. I couldn't have done it without you!

ONE

"OKAY, HOW ABOUT if I meet you at Gil's Café on Downer at eight-thirty tomorrow morning," I said. "Can you get out without anybody seeing you?"

"Yeah, I think so," Peter said in a hushed voice. "Okay, let's do it," he added after a moment's hesitation. "But *please,* Beth, don't tell anyone."

I WAS THERE AT eight-fifteen. I found a seat near the window, ordered a coffee with whipped cream, and waited and wondered. It was Monday, July 7, and Peter Barry wanted to talk to me about his father's murder. Gil's seemed like the perfect place for murder-talk. I think the quote on the menu from Raymond Chandler's *The Long Goodbye* had something to do with it. That, and the fact that it's my favorite place for breakfast.

At eight-forty, when Peter still hadn't arrived, I ordered a Holy Grail (Gil-code for endless refills of coffee). Just about the time I started to feel my heart thumping in my throat, he walked in, sat down across from me, and stared at me with his pitiful blue eyes.

"Oh, Peter," I said. "I'm so sorry."

He flicked his gaze from one corner of the room to another, and back at me.

"Beth, you have to help me," he said in a trembling voice. "You have to help me find out who killed my dad."

"Peter, the police can do a much better job than I can," I said gently. "They know it was a murder. It'll just be a matter of time before they find the killer."

"Please, Beth," he said with the most pleading look. "The cops were working on that other guy's murder, but you were the one who solved it. They never would've found that guy if it hadn't been for you."

Well, now. I had to admit he had a point. I gave him one of those Oh-gosh-I-don't-know-maybe-maybe-not looks. "Let me think about it, okay?"

He scrunched up his face, took a deep breath, and let it out. "Okay," he said.

Peter, by the way, is only sixteen years old, the neighbor boy who shovels my walk in the winter, and someone I've grown very fond of. His father, Phillip Barry, had been found murdered in the office of his accounting firm at the age of forty-seven, only three days before.

"Do you want some cocoa or some breakfast?" I said. "We can talk about it while we eat."

Peter shook his head and then nodded. "Yeah, sure," he said.

I asked for toast and orange juice and Peter ordered something approaching breakfast for two, or maybe three. I stayed off the subject for a while until he'd had quite a bit to eat, which seemed to calm him down immensely. When I thought he was ready to talk, I asked him if he had any ideas about who might have killed his father.

"Not really," he said. "But he was working on something pretty heavy for the last couple of months, staying late at the office all the time and working in the den after supper. Maybe that had something to do with it."

"How do you mean?" I asked with a frown.

"I don't know, maybe he found something out about somebody and they killed him to keep him quiet." Peter looked around to see if anyone was listening and leaned toward me across the table. "I looked through his desk in the den," he whispered, "and I took everything I could find before the cops got there."

I opened my eyes wide. "Peter, you shouldn't have done that," I said. "You really ought to give those things to the police. It might help them find the murderer."

"They're just copies," Peter said. "He always left the originals at the office. Besides, the cops wouldn't even know what to do with that stuff, but *you* will."

I smiled. "Peter, these people really are brighter than you think. One of the smartest guys from my grade school class is a Milwaukee homicide detective. They really do know what they're doing."

Peter looked at me as if I'd let him down, which made me feel pretty bad, and said, "Okay, I'll give them what I found, but not until I make my own copies, first."

I raised an eyebrow. "Well, that's a good idea," I said. "Then I can take a look at them, too."

"You mean you will help me?" Peter said, his face beaming with expectation.

"I didn't say that," I said. "I'm still thinking about it. Why don't you want anyone to know we're talking, by the way?"

"Because my mom would be super pissed off."

"Well, if I do agree to do this, we're not going to be able to keep it a secret. I'll have to talk to people your dad knew, especially your mom. That's really the only way I can get any ideas about who did it."

Peter gave me a disgruntled look. I watched his sad face and he watched mine. Sometimes I almost feel like I'm his mother. I'm certainly more than old enough to be. And I really do love him.

I gave him a determined smile. "Okay," I said. "I'll do it."

TWO

FOR THOSE OF YOU who don't know me, my name is Beth Hartley. I'm forty-three years old, unmarried (divorced once and widowed once; no children), and I run my own business doing legal research and writing for other lawyers. I'm a lawyer myself, and so is Emily Schaeffer, who has worked for me, full-time, for the last three years. I've known Emily since the fifth grade. Our secretary, Janice Grezinski, came with me when I left my law firm. Last year, her younger brother Dave was murdered, and that's how I started my brilliant mystery-solving career.

We work out of my house on the east side of Milwaukee. It's a *very* enjoyable way to make a living. None of the back-stabbing and competition you get in a law firm. We all make more than enough to live on and we usually don't have to work all that hard. I inherited the house, along with a whole ton of money, about five years ago from my Aunt Sarah. It's on Newberry Boulevard, my favorite street in the whole city, and it's absolutely enormous. Seven bedrooms, four and a half baths, three fireplaces, a four-car garage, and a real library with sliding cherry doors (where we do most of our work). There's a big yard, an interior courtyard, a screened porch in back, a side porch on the second floor, and a balcony on the third. It's made of pale Cream City brick with hunter green trim. The roof is multicolored slate and the front door is solid walnut, recessed in a little alcove and surrounded by stained, leaded glass. It really is beautiful, inside and out, and it's filled with antiques collected by my aunt. She actually left me almost everything that was in the house, including her housekeeper. Mrs. Gunther was with my Aunt Sarah for twenty-five years and now she's with me (by choice, of course). She comes in every Monday, Wednesday, and Friday, and I think of her as part of my family. I guess in some ways I think of Janice and Emily as family, too. They're certainly here often enough.

"YOU WOULDN'T BELIEVE how much Peter Barry ate for breakfast," I said to Emily and Janice when I walked into my library.

They both turned and frowned. "You had breakfast with him?" Emily said.

"Well, yeah. He didn't want me to tell anyone, but I guess it's okay now. I sort of talked him out of that."

Emily gave me one of those Huh? looks and Janice wrinkled her brow.

"He wanted to talk about his father's murder," I said casually. "But you should've seen him eat. It was ridiculous. He had this humongous omelette, potatoes, *oatmeal,* four pieces of cinnamon-sugar toast, orange juice, and two cups of cocoa."

"I guess his dad's murder didn't affect his appetite much," Emily said with an accusatory look.

Janice shrugged. "So, maybe he usually eats more."

"Oh, yeah, right," Emily said.

Janice went back to her typing, but Emily was staring at me.

"What?" I said, with a tiny edge to my voice.

"You told him you'd help him solve the murder, didn't you?"

I rolled my eyes and looked away.

"I knew it," she said.

"Well, what was I supposed to do? You should've seen his face. He would've been heartbroken if I'd said no."

"So, what, every time someone asks you to solve a murder and gives you a sad puppy dog look, you're going to say yes?"

Janice had kept her head down during Emily's and my exchange, but now she looked up, guilt and remorse clouding her face. I gave her a reassuring smile and glowered at Emily.

"No," I said, "but this is Peter. I care about him and I'm going to help him."

"You almost got yourself killed the last time."

Mrs. Gunther walked in just in time to hear that one. "What's this?" she said with a look of alarm.

I told her.

"Glory be," she said as she shook her head. "You've got a heart of gold, honey, I've always said so, but sometimes I think you don't have your head screwed on straight." She put her hands on her hips and scowled. "This is dangerous business, young lady, and you know it. Now what does Brian have to say about all this?" (Brian McHenry is the Milwaukee homicide detective with whom I went to grade school. We've sort of been seeing each other since I got involved in the first murder investigation.)

"He doesn't know about it yet," I said.

"Oh, boy, you just wait and see," Mrs. Gunther said. "He's going to give you the once-over, you mark my words."

"Well, I'm not expecting him to be happy," I said. "But I promised Peter and I'm not going back on my word."

Mrs. Gunther shook her head and left the room. I went to the library, pulled out the legal file I was working on, and went through the motions of getting to work. I had two briefs due to clients on Thursday and I'd barely begun to write. They could be hand-delivered, so there was no mail lag-time, but I still had an awful lot of work to do. As hard as I tried to concentrate, though, I couldn't get Phillip off my mind.

I actually saw him the day he died. It was in the morning, around seven o'clock, and I'd gone outside to pick up my newspaper at the same time he was retrieving his. The air was warm and dewy, and a soft breeze rustled through the trees.

"Good morning," he yelled over to me with a wave of his hand. "Looks like we're going to have a good one." He had a big grin on his face and the usual swagger to his walk. Phillip Barry was very fit and exceptionally good-looking, and he knew it.

"Hi, Phillip," I yelled back. "It sure does."

I can still see his face. He had absolutely no idea his life was going to end in only a few more hours. Late that evening, his brother Gerry found him dead on the floor of his office with a bullet wound in his chest.

After Janice, Emily, and Mrs. Gunther went home, I called Peter.

"Can you get out?" I said.

"Yeah, sure. Why?" he said.

"Did you copy that stuff yet?"

"No, I didn't get a chance."

"Okay, I'll tell you what," I said. "Bring it over here and we'll copy it on my machine. But you have to promise you'll give it to the police tomorrow, okay?"

"Okay," he said. "I'll be right over."

Well, that was disappointment number one. There wasn't a single thing there of any interest. Just a bunch of financial statements, an auditor's opinion, some kind of inventory thing, and some payroll stuff—all for one business. I read through everything, just to be sure, but nothing looked the least bit fishy or out of the ordinary. I made copies to make Peter happy and told him to give the papers to the police anyway, just in case they saw something there that I didn't.

He gave me a look of surprise.

"Well, they *are* trained to do this sort of thing and I'm not, you know. You have to remember that."

He shrugged and looked around the room.

"I'll do my best, Peter, I really will. But don't give up on the police. They may find this guy before I do, and all that really matters is that we do find him, right?"

Peter sighed and tried to smile. "Right," he said.

THE NEXT MORNING, I called Olivia (Phillip's widow and Peter's mother) and told her about Peter's request and my agreement to help him.

"I don't wish to discuss this on the telephone," she said. "Please come to the house."

Olivia is forty-six years old, so we're essentially contemporaries, but she always treats me like a child. She may not know how old I really am, but that's no excuse as far as I'm concerned. I get the impression she considers me to be beneath her "class," and she makes me feel really uncomfortable. She's very, very thin, wears a lot of beige linen and off-white silk, real furs, genuine alligator bags, and that sort of thing. Her hair is blond, all one length (about two inches below her chin), and she wears it exactly the same way all the time, turned under just a little at the edges. She has a year-round tan and really annoying, affected mannerisms. I met her mother once and she looked and acted just the same. They even have the same BMWs, only Olivia's is tan and her mother's is black.

Olivia's house is only three doors down from mine and it's really quite impressive, I'll have to admit. I was inside once before, for an "open house." It's all brick with gables everywhere and an in-ground swimming pool in the back. The living room and dining room are furnished with conservative mahogany, silk upholstery, and heavy brocade curtains. They have oil paintings with gilded frames and those little lamps on the top, and an ebony Steinway grand covered with silver-framed photographs. Their dining room table seats *sixteen.*

"Mrs. Barry is waiting in the library," Olivia's housekeeper told me when she answered the door.

I was shown to the library and had to wait a moment while the housekeeper discreetly knocked at the door. "Yes?" I heard Olivia say. After some additional formal weirdness, I was allowed to enter.

Olivia was sitting at the library desk, wearing a beige silk dress and simple gold jewelry.

"Beth, come in," she said without a smile. "Would you like tea or coffee?" Her voice indicated I'd better take one or the other.

"Coffee, please," I said. "With cream, please."

Olivia left the room for a few moments and came back. There were two dark blue leather armchairs in front of a large, ornately carved pecan desk. Olivia offered me one and she took the other. She asked me then about the health of my family and the state of my business until the housekeeper (her name is Marie, I learned later) returned with a silver service bearing coffee, cream, and sugar cubes, and a plate of biscotti with dried cranberries and pistachio nuts. After Marie poured our coffee and left, Olivia ceased the small talk.

She gave me a direct look, which lasted several awkward moments, and said, "Beth, I do not want you interfering in the investigation of my husband's death."

I gave her a tight-lipped smile.

"I realize, however, that this is important to Peter—why, I can't begin to imagine—and that he had to talk you into it. I appreciate your concern on his behalf. However," she added with emphasis, "I would prefer that you make a show of complying with his request and then leave the matter to the police. You can explain to Peter that you did what you could but that you were unable to solve the case.''

I frowned and tried to think of an appropriate response. ''Is there any particular reason you don't want me involved?'' I asked.

''Yes, there is,'' she answered. ''It is, quite simply, none of your business. Not to mention you are woefully unqualified. I would prefer the investigation be left to the experts, Beth. I want Phillip's killer found. I won't have you messing it up.''

''Olivia,'' I said, in a truly nice voice, ''I promise you I won't do anything to interfere with the police investigation. But I did tell Peter I would talk to you and the rest of the family, maybe some people from Phillip's firm, and just see if anyone knows anything.''

Olivia made no response. She added a bit of cream and one lump of sugar to her coffee, and slowly stirred it.

''Isn't there anything you can tell me?'' I said. ''Do you have any idea who might have wanted to kill him?''

She pursed her lips and put down her cup. ''I have no idea,'' she said, ''who could want Phillip dead. Now if you would...''

''What was he doing in the office that day?''

She glared at me for a moment, closed her eyes, and let out a sigh. ''Beth, if I answer your questions, will you do as I ask and let the matter drop?''

I held my breath for a moment. "I'll strongly consider it," I said.

She glared at me again, but I could see she was wearing down. "What was the question?" she said wearily.

I repeated it.

"He had some business that needed clearing up," she said, "and he insisted it couldn't wait."

"Did he say he was meeting with someone?"

"No," Olivia said. "Really, Beth. I've gone over all of this with the police."

"I'm sorry," I said. "I'm just trying to get some idea of what went on that day. Did he say he'd be back at any particular time?"

"No, he just told us to go ahead without him and he'd see us whenever he got there."

"Where were you going?" I said.

"To the Friedmans'. They're old friends and they'd invited us for the day." Olivia picked up a biscotta and took a tiny bite.

"Did he ever call there to say he'd be later than expected, or anything like that?"

Olivia sighed and put down the cookie. "No," she said quietly. "I never heard from him again." A look of pain passed across her face and she swallowed hard.

"Would you mind if I talked to the Friedmans?" I asked.

Olivia closed her eyes for a moment. "Really, Beth," she said. She was about to say something else and then she let out another sigh. "Oh, all right," she said. "I can't see what harm it can do."

"Thank you," I said.

I looked around the room for a few moments at all of Olivia's beautiful things. "Do you collect antiques yourself," I asked, "or were these passed down through your family?"

Olivia glanced around with an absentminded expression. "Oh, these were from my grandmother," she said. "On my father's side."

"They're really beautiful."

She nodded as if in a daze.

"Did Phillip have a life insurance policy?"

Now *that* woke her up. "Certainly Phillip had an insurance policy," she snapped. "Everyone does. But I can assure you, it was not a motive for murder. As you might have noticed, I was hardly in need of money before he died."

"What about the will?" I said. "Did he leave anything to anyone outside the family?"

"No. Everything went to me and to the children. Except for a few small bequests to Phillip's charities, of course."

"None of those were big enough to provide a motive?"

"I hardly think so," Olivia said. "They were no more than a couple of thousand dollars apiece."

"What about the accounting firm?" I said. "Does everything go to Gerry?"

"You'll have to discuss that with Gerry," she said. "They had some sort of an arrangement worked out."

I nodded. "What about his work or his personal life? Was he having any problems lately?"

Olivia gave me a cold, lingering stare. "Phillip and I didn't discuss his business affairs," she said. "They were confidential. You, of all people, should understand that."

I sighed and willed myself to be calm. "Would you mind my asking how you and Phillip met?" I said then.

Olivia's face softened a bit. "We met through my father," she said. "Both our fathers, really. My father and Win, Phillip's father, were business colleagues for many years. I think they decided very early on that we were a suitable match."

I gave her a weak smile. She looked suddenly sad and tired.

"Do you know if Phillip had any problems with anyone?" I asked. "Did he have any enemies? Was anyone angry with him?"

Olivia put down her cup again and stared out the window. Shafts of light shone through and illuminated the dust in the air. "No," was all she said, after a long pause.

"Well, I do appreciate your talking to me," I said. She didn't respond.

"Olivia," I said gently. "I promise I won't cause you any trouble. I'll explain to everyone I talk to that I'm just doing this for Peter. I'm sure they'll understand."

No answer again.

"Would it be all right with you if I talk to Haley

and Paul? I promise to keep it short and I won't talk to them until after the funeral."

Olivia turned to me with tears in her eyes, and nodded. She looked at me steadily for a few moments. "I know you're only trying to help, Beth. I'm sorry if I was rude. This hasn't been easy on any of us."

I felt a rush of pity and warmth toward her, along with a bit of guilt. She's a real snot, but I still felt sorry for her.

"Don't apologize," I said. "I'm the one who should be sorry. I know this is a rough time for you and I never would have interfered if Peter hadn't asked me to. It really seems to mean a lot to him, though. He's convinced I'll be able to solve it even if the police can't, because I solved that other murder."

"I read about that," Olivia said, looking genuinely impressed (okay, maybe not). "You have a lot of courage."

I laughed. "Either that or I'm crazy, right?"

"Right," she said with a hint of a smile.

Olivia stood up, which I guessed meant I was leaving, so I stood up, too. "I'll give you a call," she said, "when I've talked to Paul and Haley. I'll let you know when it would be convenient for you to see them."

"Thank you," I said. "That would be great." I hesitated at the door. "You don't mind if I come to the funeral, do you?"

Olivia frowned at me. "Goodness, no," she said. "Beth, really. I apologize for putting you off. Please don't feel unwelcome. We would be grateful if you could come. Peter, particularly. The wake is tonight, of course.''

"Thanks,'' I said with a smile. "I'll be there.''

THREE

IT WAS A beautiful day, with a deep blue sky, full,
fluffy clouds, temperatures in the seventies, and birds
chirping merrily. I opened my kitchen windows when
I got home, poked my head in the library to tell Janice
and Emily I was back, and sat down at my kitchen
table to start a "Phillip" file. I wrote down everything
Olivia had told me—which was essentially nothing—
and did the same for Peter. After that, I made a list
of the people I knew I wanted to talk to, relying pri-
marily on what I had learned from Peter.

Phillip and Olivia had three children, Peter, Paul,
and Haley. Paul is the oldest, at twenty, Haley is nineteen, and Peter, sixteen. Both Phillip's father and
mother are dead. He had one sister, Audrey, and a
brother, Gerry, both younger than he. Audrey is married to a lawyer, Richard, and they have two sons.
Gerry is married to Sue, a nurse, and they have a girl
and a boy. Phillip and Gerry were both CPAs and
opened an accounting firm together shortly after their
father died. In addition to the two of them, there were
several secretaries and at least one more CPA at the
firm. Peter wasn't sure how many. I'd need to talk to
all of them, as well as the Friedmans. I closed the file,
went into the library, and put it away.

I worked until five, when Janice and Emily went
home, had an early supper of fruit salad and iced tea,

and went upstairs to get ready for Phillip's wake. I opened my closet and groaned. I had nothing to wear. I look hideous in black, all of my old courtroom suits (which work even better for funerals) were too hot, and my dark blue cocktail dress just wasn't quite it. I finally settled on a navy knit dress and gold earrings, my hair on top of my head. It would have to do.

I DROVE TO Capitol Drive, where the funeral home is located, then drove around for fifteen minutes trying to find a parking place because the lot was full. I walked in at twenty after seven and wriggled my way through the crowd. Phillip's wake was remarkably well attended, but still the usual gloomy gathering. Quiet voices, no laughing, serious looks, and somber greetings. It took me more than ten minutes to find Peter, who looked immeasurably grateful to see me when I did. He pointed out a few of his relatives, a couple of Phillip's colleagues, and introduced me to Anna Schulz (Phillip's secretary), and to Phillip's brother, Gerry. Gerry was polite and kind, and willingly agreed to talk with me anytime after the funeral.

"Just call the office," he said.

One of the CPAs from the firm, a woman named Sharon Falk, came over and gave her condolences to Peter. Peter introduced me and told her I was helping to investigate Phillip's death. She raised her eyebrows, extended her hand, and said, "Are you with the police department?"

I explained that I wasn't, and she raised her eyebrows again. Then she said "Excuse me," and walked away.

Peter gave me a look of apology. "She used to be nicer before her daughter got killed," he said.

"Oh, my gosh," I said with a wince. "When did that happen?"

"Last Christmas," he said. "It was a car accident but Mrs. Falk was driving so my mom says she feels like it was her fault so we shouldn't blame her for being crabby."

I smiled and nodded. It seemed an uncharacteristically sensitive thing for Olivia to say. Maybe she wasn't such a bad person after all.

Olivia and her mother were there, of course, both quite appropriately dressed in black linen, but they'd abandoned their usual hairstyle. This time, they wore it pulled back quite severely and secured by gold clasps. Haley, to my great surprise, was wearing red. It was an elegant red crepe dress but still, very, very red. I saw her grandmother give her a disapproving look more than once. Olivia practically ignored her.

Paul, the oldest of the three children, wore a dark gray pin-striped suit, white dress shirt, rep tie, and wing-tip shoes. He looked kind of ridiculous, like a kid playing dress up. The expression on his face was cold and hard.

Although the room was quite crowded, I didn't see anyone who looked guilty or the least bit suspicious. I wasn't really paying much attention, though. Peter stayed close to me all evening and seemed almost to panic if I so much as stepped away. I kept with him until it was over, and even drove him home. Olivia didn't seem to care one way or the other. She wasn't being very motherly, I thought, but then, she had just lost her husband.

The funeral was the next morning, at St. John's Roman Catholic Cathedral on North Jackson Street. A marvelous church, with the loveliest stained-glass windows. The man sitting next to me told me it has a baldachino over the altar. I have no idea what that is.

I couldn't sit with Peter (Olivia wouldn't let me), and I wasn't allowed to stand near him at the cemetery, either. Olivia's invitation to the house was so perfunctory and cool I was tempted to decline, but Peter begged me to come, so I did. I stayed for over an hour, and when Peter said he wanted to go upstairs and lie down, I went home.

Mrs. Gunther, Emily, and Janice were at the house when I got there. I poked my head into the library and said hello to Janice and Emily, then went to the kitchen to make a cup of tea. Emily followed me.

"How was the funeral?" she said.

"Peter was miserable," I said with a sigh.

"How about the wife?"

"Didn't shed a tear."

Emily raised an eyebrow.

"Well, that doesn't necessarily mean anything," I said. "Neither did Haley or Paul."

"Who are they?"

"Peter's brother and sister."

I got a mug from the cupboard, filled it with water, and put it in the microwave. Emily was eyeing me curiously. "What?" I said (as in "What the heck are you looking at?").

"Nothing," she said. "So, what have you found out so far? Do you have any idea who did it?"

I put a tea bag in my cup and grinned. "You're really interested in this, aren't you?"

She gave me a snotty look.

"Well, you are, I can tell. You want to know who did it as much as I do."

"Okay, fine. Don't tell me," she snapped, and left the room.

I laughed. "I didn't find anything out yet," I yelled after her.

THE NEXT DAY, Olivia called—quite early—to talk about my interviewing her children.

"Haley's day off is Monday," she said. "If you wish, you can come and talk to her then." Olivia's voice wasn't unfriendly, but it was flat, sort of lifeless. Not surprising, I guess, for the day after her husband's funeral. I wanted to say something consoling but I felt uneasy about it, so I didn't.

"That would be great," I said instead. "Thanks, Olivia. What time would be good for her?"

"How about three?" she said. "Is that all right?"

"Perfect," I said. "Thanks."

"I haven't talked to Paul yet," she said then. "I'll have to let you know about him."

"That's fine," I said. "Tell Haley I'll see her on Monday and I'll try to keep it short. I promise."

"Thank you, Beth," Olivia said, and she hung up.

Now wasn't she being cooperative?

Janice arrived shortly after that. She came into the

kitchen and poured herself a cup of coffee. "How's Peter?" she asked with an anxious look.

"He's taking it pretty hard," I said.

Janice nodded, and suddenly looked close to tears.

I frowned. "This is bringing back bad memories for you, isn't it?"

She looked at me with moist eyes and nodded again.

"Oh, gosh, I'm sorry," I said. "Maybe, if you feel up to it sometime, you and Peter could talk. It might help you both to have someone to talk to who went through the same thing."

Janice gave me a weak smile. "Yeah, maybe," she said. "Do you think he'd want to talk to me?"

"I'm sure he would," I said. "He's always liked you."

For some reason, that made Janice start crying.

"Oh, I'm sorry," I said again.

"That's okay," she said. "It's just that he kind of reminds me of Dave."

I couldn't see how, but I just smiled in response.

I waited ten minutes more, until Emily arrived, and told them both I was going to deliver my briefs and do some research at Marquette University. "There's pasta-vegetable salad and chicken soup in the refrigerator," I said, "in case I don't get back."

"Homemade?" Janice asked with a wistful look.

"Of course," I said.

I gathered everything I needed, filled my briefcase, and headed downtown. I took the scenic route, my favorite drive along Lake Michigan. The day was warm and sunny again, almost eighty degrees, the sky a clear deep blue. There was only a bit of wind and the sun glistened off the ripples on the lake. Morning joggers and speed-walkers moved along the shoreline path, children were already playing on the beach, and the sea gulls swooped and soared. I opened my window, breathed in the fresh air, and smiled to myself. I actually know people (not from Milwaukee, of course) who think very little of Lake Michigan, insisting that nothing can compare to an ocean. It's just not true. Lake Michigan is so beautiful, and it's different, every single day. Each time I drive by that lake, the water is a different color, a different mood. At times, it's almost perfectly still, with just a hint of movement, and the sun reflects off the surface with a silvery sheen. Then, within hours, a storm can brew and the water turns black and angry, the waves powerful and relentless as they crash against the shore. It's truly fascinating to watch, even frightening, but in the most exciting way. I think my favorite time of all is in the late afternoon when the sky is washed with subtle and delicate color, the sea gulls fly for the sheer joy of it, and white sails beckon far off in the distance. It's simply lovely. I feel so lucky to live near the lake.

MY FIRST STOP WAS the Firstar Center on East Wisconsin Avenue (formerly the First Wisconsin Building). This was Milwaukee's first skyscraper, and the only one we had for many years. I parked in the lot across from the building, took the elevator to the highest heights, delivered the brief to the receptionist in the lobby, retrieved my car, and headed for the

Reuss Federal Plaza, across from the Boston Store. You can't miss this one. It's the color of a milk-of-magnesia bottle.

I dropped off the second brief and drove to Marquette. I went to law school there and Emily and I use the law library for our research. I bought a cup of coffee from the machine downstairs, found a carrel with no trouble at all, and got right to work. I researched straight through until three o'clock without even stopping for lunch, picked up a sandwich from Grebe's Bakery across the street when I was done, and ate as I drove home.

"Olivia called," Emily said when I walked in.

"Brian called, too," Janice said in a teasing voice. She and Emily looked at each other and grinned.

"What is your problem?" I said, trying not to laugh.

"Hey, if you don't want us to know all the intimate details of your personal telephonic life, you shouldn't have your answering machine in the same room with us," Emily said with one of those "Ha, ha" smiles of hers. "Either that, or fix it so we don't hear the messages."

I looked at her sideways. "Maybe I'll do that," I said.

I went to the kitchen and called Olivia back. "I've talked to Paul," she said. "He works all week, of course, but he will see you tonight, if that's convenient."

I was more than mildly surprised. "Sure," I said. "That would be great. What time did you have in mind?"

"Seven-fifteen?"

"That's great," I said. "Tell Paul I'll see him then. And thanks, Olivia."

I hung up the phone and frowned. She was being a little too helpful, from my perspective. When I'd first talked to her, she didn't want me involved at all, and now she was practically planning the investigation for me. Very strange.

Brian's message (in addition to the part that gave Janice and Emily such a thrill) was that he'd be out of town until Friday but back in time for our dinner date that night, so I had no reason to call him back. I joined Janice and Em in the library, worked until they went home at five, and then brought everything into the kitchen and wrote for another hour. I had four briefs due to clients by the next week, and Emily had three. I'd completed two of mine over a week ago and I wanted the third one out of the way by Monday. That would save Janice from the nearly impossible task of typing more than half a dozen briefs in one week. I have one computer, and, as of a few months ago, a word processor. I use the word processor in times of emergency for a temporary typist so I can have two tapping away at the same time. I don't know why I didn't think of that sooner.

At six, I made myself some rye toast and an omelette with sweet peppers and onions, and then relaxed for a bit, trying to decide what I wanted to ask Paul. After I finished eating, I got out my Phillip file, brought it into the kitchen, and made a few notes while I drank my after-dinner tea.

At seven-ten, I walked over to Olivia's house.

FOUR

OLIVIA ANSWERED the door herself. She gave me her usual cool regard, but she was fidgeting with her rings.

"Paul's in the library," she said. She led me there, opened the doors, and stood back to let me pass. I was looking at Paul when I walked in. He looked over my shoulder with a pointed glare until the doors closed behind me.

He was sitting at his father's desk with some papers spread before him. Paul is tall, like his father was— about six feet—and he has Phillip's dark hair but his mother's bright green eyes. The combination is actually a little eerie. He was wearing a white dress shirt with gold cufflinks. He didn't smile or say hello, just tightened his jaw and stared. Kind of a creepy stare for a twenty-year-old. I'd met him before, of course, but I'd never gotten to know him like I know Peter. He'd never shown any interest, anyway.

"Hi, Paul," I said a little uncomfortably.

He nodded his head, ever so slightly, but didn't speak.

"I hope you don't mind talking to me," I said. "I don't know if your mother told you, but I'm doing this as a favor to Peter."

Still no response, but his neck and face turned a light red.

"It might help if you talk to me," I said. "We might be able to come up with something."

He sighed and looked away. For some reason, I took that as encouragement.

"That's all right," I said. "I understand. You don't have to talk to me if you don't want to. If you change your mind, though, let me know, okay?"

I turned to leave and was almost at the door when he finally spoke.

"Wait," he said, so quietly I barely heard him.

I turned and looked at him.

"I'll talk to you now," he said.

I came forward and sat down in one of the chairs in front of the desk. "It really is all right if you don't want to," I said. And I really meant it.

Paul snorted a laugh. "Not with my mother, it isn't."

"I'll try to keep it short," I said. "I just want to know if you have any ideas about who killed your father."

He shrugged with one shoulder. "I don't know who killed him," he said. His voice was dull and lifeless, just like his face.

"Do you know if anyone was angry with him for either personal or professional reasons?"

He shrugged again. "No," was all he said. I couldn't decide if he was being cooperative or not.

"Did you ever hear him arguing or fighting with anyone?"

He hesitated just a moment before he answered that one. "No," he said. "I never heard anything like that."

"You don't know of anyone who might have had a grudge against him? Someone who was upset with him about something?"

He hesitated again, and looked away. "No, I don't," he said.

"Do you have any ideas at all about who killed your father?"

He shook his head.

Boy, this was a fruitful discussion. "Well, okay," I said. "If you do think of something later, would you let me know?"

"Sure," he said under his breath.

"Thanks, Paul," I said. "Don't worry, they'll find your father's murderer, I'm sure of it. And I'm going to do everything I can to help."

He lowered his eyes and made no response.

I had my hand on the door when I turned around and said, "Oh, one more question. You're an accounting major, right?"

He nodded without looking up.

"Were you planning to join your father's firm after you graduate?"

Paul raised his head and gave me a rather sharp look. It only lasted a moment, but it was long enough. "Yes," he said quickly. I nodded and let myself out.

Olivia was loitering in the hallway when I came out of the library. "Was he helpful?" she asked me.

"No, not really," I said. "He doesn't have any idea who could have done it and he doesn't know of anyone who had a grudge against him, either."

Olivia gave me a strange look, one I really couldn't read. Relief? Disappointment? Concern?

"Well, thanks, Olivia," I said. "I'll see you on Monday."

She nodded and let me out. "Good night, Beth," she said in a tired voice.

I walked home feeling like I'd accomplished nothing. I'd spoken to two of Phillip's family members now, in addition to Peter, and neither of them knew a thing.

The next morning, I called Gerry's office. "Barry, Barry and Associates," a woman said.

"May I speak to Gerry Barry?" I said. (Nice name, huh?)

"One moment, please," the woman said, and I was transferred to another line. I told the woman on that line who I was and why I was calling, learned that she was Gerry's personal secretary, and was told that Gerry could see me on Monday at two, or Tuesday at four, if either was convenient for me.

"Tuesday at four would be great," I said.

Then I called Olivia.

"Olivia," I said. "It's Beth Hartley."

I heard her sigh.

"I was wondering if you could give me the Friedmans' number."

Another sigh. "Just a moment," she said.

A minute later she was back on the phone, gave me the number in a grudging tone of voice, and asked me to please keep in mind who I was talking to. Now what the heck was that supposed to mean?

I dialed the number as soon as I hung up. A maid of some sort answered the phone and summoned Mrs.

Friedman. I explained the situation to her as succinctly as I could and asked if I could meet with her sometime within the next few days. She sounded a bit put off at first, but she agreed to see me at four that same afternoon.

I worked until one-thirty, had a black bean and tortilla casserole for lunch with Janice, Em, and Mrs. G (I know it sounds weird, but it's really good—lots of cheese and green onions and black olives), worked for another hour, said good-bye, and took off.

The Friedmans live *in a mansion* on Lake Drive, in Fox Point. You'd have to see this place to believe it. The five-car garage is bigger than the house I grew up in. The greenhouse is even bigger. They have a formal garden with benches, a gazebo, and a waterfall. The foyer has a white marble floor, gold embossed wall coverings, and a gleaming brass railing on a broad, winding staircase. I took a peek at the ballroom (just to the left of the elevator) before I was shown to the parlor to wait for Mrs. Friedman. The parlor was about the same size as my living room, with French doors, brocade curtains in a light olive color, and matching sofas covered in a slightly darker shade of olive with gold braiding and shiny brass tacks all around the edges. Two wing chairs in a subtle gold and green stripe. Mahogany tables. The maid ushered me in without a word and closed the doors. She was wearing a black uniform with a white organdy apron. So were the *other two* maids I saw in the hallway.

Several minutes later, Mrs. Friedman appeared. She was small, maybe five-four or-five, with soft gray hair worn in a loose knot at the top of her head, and large, deep-set, blue eyes. She wasn't overly thin, but she was fit and healthy-looking, and her makeup was subtle and elegant. She wore a slim-fitting, light blue knit dress and gray flats, and she gave me a smile when she walked in. It wasn't a particularly warm one, but it wasn't cool and aloof like Olivia's, either.

"Miss Hartley?" she said, as she extended her hand. "I'm Nicole Friedman. Please, sit down."

I sat.

I was just about to say something when a maid appeared with a coffee and tea tray. "Thank you, Constance," Nicole said to the woman. "That will be all."

The maid nodded without looking at either of us and left the room. "Would you care for coffee or tea?" Nicole asked.

"Coffee would be fine," I said. "Thank you."

We went through the usual one-lump-or-two and cream routine, then settled down to talk.

"Now tell me," Nicole said. "What can I do for you?" She leaned back against the couch with her legs crossed and took a sip of coffee. She intrigued me, somehow. She was cool, but friendly; refined, but casual. No real pretense, I decided.

I'd already explained my involvement in the case when we'd talked on the phone, so I got right to the point. "Did Phillip call here on the day he died, either before or after Olivia arrived?"

"No, he didn't," Nicole said. "I only talked to Olivia. She called that morning to say that Phillip might be late but that she and the children would be here at eleven.''

"What had you planned for the day?" I asked.

"Nothing special," Nicole said. "A little tennis, a barbecue, swimming. The usual."

"So it was just supposed to be a leisurely day with nothing formal planned for any particular time?"

"Exactly," Nicole said. Then she frowned. "What is it that concerns you, specifically?"

"Well, nothing, really. I'm just trying to get a sense of the day Phillip had planned. If he'd arranged to be here for a formal dinner, for example, he would have had to be here at a particular time."

"Oh, I see," she said. She took a sip of coffee, set down the cup, and looked at me with a bland expression.

"Did Olivia seem nervous or not herself at anytime during the day?"

"Not at all," Nicole said. "We sat by the pool most of the afternoon and sipped margaritas. Actually," she added with a slightly guilty look, "we were both quite pleased that our husbands *weren't* here. It gave us a chance to chat, like old times."

"So you've known Olivia for a long time?"

"Since high school," Nicole said. "We were both at St. Mary's Academy. I was a year ahead of Olivia, but we had an art class together and became fast friends."

I grinned. "I didn't know Olivia went to St. Mary's," I said. "I went there, too."

"You did?" Nicole said. "What class were you in?"

"Nineteen seventy-one."

Nicole raised her eyebrows. "My, you certainly hide your age well," she said.

"Thanks," I said with a smile.

"Did all three of the children come with Olivia?" I suddenly thought to ask.

"Only Haley and Peter," Nicole said. "Paul had another engagement."

I wondered about that for just a moment, but then I told myself I was being overly suspicious. "Do you have any idea what his other engagement was?"

Nicole shrugged. "Just a date, I imagine."

I nodded. "Did any of them express any concern during the day about where Phillip was?"

Nicole sighed and didn't answer right away. Both our cups were empty by then so she refilled them and waited until I'd added cream to mine. "You have to understand something about Phillip and Olivia," she said then.

"Olivia was used to being abandoned by Phillip. And disappointed, and ignored. She grew to expect very little from him. When he didn't show up, I'm sure she thought nothing of it."

"What about Haley and Peter?" I said.

"I'm sure the same was true for them," Nicole said. "They must have been used to Phillip's ways."

"How long did they stay?"

"Five, maybe a little later."

"And no mention was ever made of Phillip."

Nicole frowned and put down her cup. "Not that I recall," she said. She gazed through the French doors into the garden, and was silent for several moments. "We didn't hear of his death until the next day," she said, her eyes still focused on the garden. "I understand his brother discovered the body."

"Yes," I said. "When he hadn't come home and didn't answer Olivia's calls, she finally became concerned and asked Gerry to check on him."

"There, you see," Nicole said as she turned to look at me again. "She *was* concerned after sufficient time had passed to warrant it. You have to put this in perspective. Phillip rarely spent anytime with Olivia, and he had a habit of breaking whatever arrangements he did make with her. It was different in the beginning, of course, but things change between people after so many years. They grow apart. They adjust." She stopped and looked out at the flowers again.

"You have a beautiful garden," I said, but I'm not sure she heard me. She looked perplexed and disturbed somehow. Preoccupied.

"Well, I guess I'll be going," I said then, but she still wasn't listening. I stood up and she turned around. "Thank you very much for talking to me," I said. "You've been very helpful."

She smiled and walked me out. "You're quite welcome," she said. "I hope you'll keep me informed of your progress."

The request caught me by surprise, but I agreed to call her should I have anything worthwhile to report.

I MADE MY USUAL notations in the Phillip file when I got home, had a cup of tea and an apple, and took a long, hot shower. I was seeing Brian that night and I was truly dreading it. I'd missed him like crazy since

I last saw him but there was no way I could avoid telling him about my involvement in Phillip's murder investigation. If he found out from someone else, I don't think he'd ever forgive me, and he was sure to find out, sooner or later. Even hearing it from me, he was going to be furious.

I decided my best defense was *distraction.* I took forever putting on my makeup, did my nails, put on a pale pink knit dress Brian nearly died over the first time I wore it, and even set my hair. I figured if I looked *really good* he might just forget to get angry with me. Yeah, right.

"Hey," Brian said when I opened the door. "You look gorgeous." He put his arms around me and gave me a long, lingering hug. Then he looked at me with a seductive smile, still holding on to my waist. "So, what have you been up to lately?"

"Nothing," I said, sounding way too defensive.

He frowned and gave me a funny look.

I almost told him, right then, but I decided to wait until later. No point in ruining the *entire* evening. Brian had been working on some big, secret case that had kept him so busy we hadn't really seen each other for the last three months. It was finally over, and this was the first weekend night we'd had together in a long time.

"Is Mader's okay?" he said when we pulled away from the curb.

"Are you kidding?" I said. "I love that place. It's like eating in a real castle."

Brian laughed and brushed his fingers across my cheek. "I really missed you, you know that?" he said.

"I missed you, too," I said with a knot in my stomach.

Mader's, in case you don't know, is one of Milwaukee's finest German restaurants. The city is, in very large part, a city of Germans, and we have a lot of really good German restaurants to show for it. At the beginning of the century, nearly three-fourths of the population was German-born or of German descent. There's much more of a mix now—in fact the city is quite ethnically diverse—but German and Polish are still the dominant populations.

Mader's is on Old World Third Street, a somewhat preserved section of the former German-American commercial district. Usinger's Sausage, Ambrosia Chocolate, The Spice House, and The Wisconsin Cheese Mart are among the favorite survivors. It's a charming little corner of town, but I do miss the cobblestone streets. They paved them over a few years ago, and a good deal of charm went along with them. Mader's still looks like an old castle, though, with turrets and battlements, arched doorways, suits of armor, swords and shields. I feel like I'm in another world when I'm inside, and I never want to leave.

We left the car with the valet, sat at the bar for a while until we were shown to our table, and spent at least ten awkward minutes perusing the menu and commenting on the decor. It was ridiculous. We'd been there at least half a dozen times and Brian always orders the same thing. Something was bothering me, and he knew it. And I knew he knew it. I didn't say a word about it, though, through the entire dinner. But when we got back to my house, and I handed him a brandy and coffee, he said, "Beth, is something bothering you?" A worried and slightly pained expression crossed his face.

"No, it's nothing," I said. "I just…"

He frowned and looked even more anxious. "You just what?" he said.

"I just have something to tell you that I don't think you're going to like."

Now I got a wary look, almost entirely displacing the anxious one.

I took a deep breath and let it out. "I'm involved in another murder investigation," I said.

Brian closed his eyes and leaned his head against the back of the couch. After a few long moments, he said, "It's the Barry murder, right?"

"Right," I said. "Peter Barry's his sixteen-year-old son. He shovels snow for me and I know him really well and he asked me to help. I just couldn't say no."

Brian removed his glasses and rubbed his eyes with one hand. He sighed and put them back on. "Beth," he said in a weary voice, "I don't know what to say. If I tell you to stay out of it, you'll just tell me you can't break a promise."

"Well, I'm glad you understand," I said.

He didn't look at me, but I could see him tighten his jaw. "If I tell you," he said after a moment's hesitation, "that you're interfering with a police investigation, you'll say the police need your help, since, as you so often put it, they never could have solved the Grezinski case without you."

"Well…"

"And if I tell you it's dangerous, you'll say you'll be careful."

"But..."

"Stay out of it, Beth."

"I thought you weren't going to say that," I said, not bothering to hide my annoyance.

Brian's neck and face got red. "Beth, I'm ordering you to stay out of it."

"You order me to stay out of it," I said. "What are you going to do, take away my P.I.'s license? I don't have one. You can't arrest me, I'm not breaking any laws. So, what are you going to do, Brian?"

Brian clenched his teeth, put down his brandy glass with a thud, and stood up. "I'm going to leave, Beth. That's what I'm going to do."

And he walked out the door, just like that.

THE NEXT DAY was Saturday, and I woke up feeling really depressed. I didn't want Brian angry with me. I wanted him to call me and tell me how wonderful he thinks I am, like he usually does. What he really ought to have done is *thank* me. After all, I was helping him, and his department, by doing some of their work for them. Men are always so ungrateful.

I worked on my brief on and off the whole day, and jumped every time I heard the phone. Brian and I almost always do something together on Saturday nights, but he didn't even call. I stayed up late and precooked a dinner to bring to Mrs. Robinson's house, a sweet old woman I met during the Dave Grezinski murder investigation. We have dinner together every Sunday night now. I usually make something at home and just heat it up later in her oven. This time it was baked mostociolli, an Italian salad, and blueberry pie for dessert (all her request). When I'd finished my baking and cleaned everything up, I got into bed and read until almost two, still hoping he'd call, and finally turned out the light.

I GOT UP LATE Sunday morning, feeling groggy and headachy, had a small breakfast of toast, tea, and fruit, and worked on my brief (uninterrupted by any phone calls from you-know-whom) until it was time to leave for Mrs. Robinson's.

Mrs. Robinson lives in an old, once-elegant-and-stately apartment building just off of Brady Street. It's the same building Dave Grezinski (Janice's brother) lived and died in. Mrs. Robinson's apartment was right next door to his. I worried myself half to death over her during that investigation, afraid Dave's killer would harm her, too, for fear she'd seen or heard something. She had, and still has, a habit of keeping her door wide open.

"Hello-o," I said through that open door when I arrived fifteen minutes later. She was sitting in her favorite chair with the tiny-flowered upholstery and decorative doilies, nodding off, but not quite asleep.

"Beth, dear," she said in a sleepy voice, and attempted to get up.

"That's all right, don't get up," I said. I walked over and gave her a kiss and a hug. "I'll be right back. I have to make one more trip."

I went back down and got the remainder of my provisions, brought everything into the kitchen, and lighted the oven. I put the mostociolli in on low and then heated some water for tea in the microwave I bought her for her eighty-seventh birthday, in April. We had the nicest little party. Just Mrs. Robinson, I, and Mrs. Markham, another nice woman down the hall.

I brought the tea in on a tray and put it on the coffee table.

"Beth, dear," she said. "You are an angel."

I smiled and handed her a cup. After she'd taken a few sips and set it down on the table beside her chair, she said, "Now tell me all about your week. I want to know everything you've been doing."

"Well, I'm involved in another murder investigation," I said excitedly.

"Oh, my dear," she said, just as excitedly. "Tell me all about it."

I told her what had transpired so far, including my fight with Brian.

"He'll come around," she said. "You'll see."

"I don't know," I said. "He seemed pretty upset."

"Well, he's acting mighty foolish, then. He'll never find another girl as wonderful as you."

"Thanks," I said with an appreciative smile. "You always make me feel so much better."

"That's what good friends are for, my dear."

I got up and gave her a hug. "Are you ready for dinner yet?" I asked.

"Oh, my, yes," she said. "I've been waiting all day for your wonderful cooking."

We had a splendid dinner as always—Mrs. Robinson raved about every little thing—and I stayed until around seven so we could chat.

"Now I want you to keep me posted on your investigation," she said in a conspiratorial whisper. "I want to know everything that happens."

"Don't worry, I will," I said with a laugh, and I gave her a good-bye hug and kiss. "I'll see you next week."

When I got home, I checked my messages in the hope that Brian had called, but he hadn't. Well, at least I had one thing to look forward to the next day. I was seeing Haley at three o'clock, and that was sure to be entertaining. As it turned out, it was quite enlightening, too.

FIVE

"WHAT'S THE MATTER with you?" Emily said when she walked in the next morning.

"Oh, nothing," I said in a crabby voice. "Brian's not talking to me."

"I told you he'd be mad if you started messing around with another murder investigation. What did you expect?" She had a look on her face that I could have sworn was satisfaction.

"He'll get over it," I said, feeling not at all certain of that. Emily gave me one of those Yes - you - just - go - right - ahead - and - believe - that - if - it - makes - you - feel - better smiles.

I was seeing Haley at three that afternoon and I still had two issues left on the killer brief. They were difficult ones, too, requiring a lot of time-consuming transcript references and argument by analogy. It's my favorite kind of work, to be honest, because it's more of a challenge, but I really wasn't in the mood that day. I talked to Mrs. Gunther for a few minutes, chatted a little more with Emily and Janice, and then forced myself to work. At one-fifteen, when I'd completed one of the issues, I stopped for lunch and suggested we order out from William Ho's (they deliver). Everyone was agreeable, so we shared two orders of chicken almond ding with brown rice and a large shrimp fried rice. After ingesting a bit too much food and way too much tea, I was back at work. I kept at it until ten to three, had another cup of tea, and ran down the street to see Haley.

I was informed by Olivia, when I arrived, that Haley would see me in her bedroom. I was a little irritated by that at first, but then I decided it might be kind of interesting to get a peek at her inner sanctum—and I was right.

Haley's room is on the second floor, the fourth one down, at the end of a long and wide, plushly carpeted corridor. Olivia walked me up, waited for me to knock, and moved discreetly away (though I caught her taking a curious peek back at me when she reached the top of the stairs).

"Come in," I heard Haley say.

I walked into a room larger than most of the master bedrooms they put in new houses nowadays. It had some sort of really ornate crown molding, painted white like the ceiling, and textured wallpaper in a robin's-egg blue. The paper had a raised design that reminded me of old plaster trim or scrollwork. The floor was highly polished hardwood, covered almost completely by an Oriental-type rug in shades of blue, rose, and light green. Her bedspread (on what looked to be a king-sized bed) was pure white, a beautifully embossed brocade. The curtains were sheer white chiffon with billowing ruffles. Her bed was a poster bed, just like the kind every girl I ever knew wanted when we were growing up. It even had a canopy. There was a matching cherry armoire and dresser, a little vanity with a chair and a ruffled skirt, a writing desk, a cedar hope chest, a lingerie chest, and an oversized armchair upholstered in white fabric with a tiny pale blue and light green flowered print. The chair had a ruffle, too, along the bottom. The whole thing was a bit overdone, to put it mildly, but I still found it enviable.

Haley was sitting at the vanity, filing her nails. She glanced up with a bored look she'd probably practiced and went back to what she was doing.

"Hi, Haley," I said. "I hope you don't mind talking to me. I promise I won't take too long."

She shrugged and made a face to go with it. "No problem," she said. "I'm not going anywhere."

I smiled an amused smile she didn't see. She hadn't asked me to sit down, but I did anyway, in the upholstered chair. Next to me, on the dresser, was a pile of neatly folded and pressed clothes. Haley went on to the next nail, paying absolutely no attention to me. For some reason, though, I was more fascinated than annoyed. Everything about her exuded privilege and luxury. She was wearing slim-fitting, dark green linen slacks and a matching silk blouse. It looked beautiful—striking, really—next to her pale blond hair. She had diamond studs in her ears, probably a carat each (of course, they could have been cubic zirconia, but somehow I doubted it). She wore her hair all one length like her mother's, only a bit longer, the ends turned under and nearly touching her shoulders. She reminded me a little of Grace Kelly, except that her manners weren't as refined.

She finished her nail job, put the file away, and moved over to her desk, still acting as if I weren't even there. She removed a cloth napkin from a silver tray I'd only just noticed, and placed it in her lap.

"Have you eaten?" she said, as she scanned the tray.

"Yes, thanks," I said. "Don't let me interrupt your lunch, though."

She glanced over at me, gave me a solicitous smile, and popped a piece of cheddar cheese in her mouth. In addition to the cheese, the tray held slices of rare roast beef, brown mustard in a small pot, some sort of pickled or marinated vegetable salad with tomatoes, red onions, green peppers, and cucumbers, and a little two-cup infuser of coffee with a small pitcher of cream. The cup was fine china. Real silver, too.

"Mother says you want to talk to me about Daddy," she said as she speared a forkful of salad.

"Did she tell you why?" I said.

"Well, I assume it's about the murder," Haley said.

"Yes, it is," I said, "but I mean did she tell you about Peter?"

Haley turned and stared at me. "What about him?"

"I just meant that I'm doing this as a favor to him. He asked me to see if I can figure out who killed your father and I told him I'd talk to all of you and see what I can come up with."

"Oh," she said, and let out a breath. "Well, whatever."

"Do you mind talking about it?" I asked.

She poured a small amount of coffee into her fine china cup and added a bit of cream. "No," she said with a sigh. "You're the first person who *has* talked to me about it. Everyone else just walks around here like nothing happened—or like *something* happened but it's something you're not supposed to talk about.''

I gave her a sympathetic smile. ''Well, sometimes people just don't know what to say, so they don't say anything at all.''

''I guess,'' Haley said. ''Do you think you know who killed my dad?''

''Oh, no,'' I said. ''Not yet, anyway. I've really only talked to your mother and Paul, and neither of them seem to have any idea who might have done it.''

She looked about to say something, but she didn't.

''Do you think you know who might have killed him?'' I asked.

Haley cut a bite-sized bit of beef, spread a little mustard on it, and put it in her mouth. She took her time about it, chewed slowly, and swallowed.

''Well, as far as I can figure it,'' she said, ''it was probably one of his many jilted mistresses.''

I stared at her, my eyes opened wide. She saw my reaction and smiled slightly, as if she were pleased with the effect. She removed a silver cigarette box from a desk drawer, took out a cigarette, and lit it with one of those big clunky silver lighters. She held the cigarette poised, in a really affected manner, and blew the smoke right at me. ''He'd been fooling around on Mom for years,'' she said, in an I'm-sophisticated-and-worldly-and-none-of-this-shocks-me sort of way. ''Everyone knew it.''

''Did your mom know?''

''She knew,'' Haley said.

"Do you think your dad knew she knew?"

"I doubt it," she said with a shrug. "Mom's the silent, suffering type. Besides, it'd be too humiliating to acknowledge it."

I sighed. "Why would she want to stay with him?"

"Look around," Haley said, waving a hand. "Why do you think she stayed?"

"Yeah, but your mom comes from a family with money, too. She wouldn't need to be married to your father to live like this."

"So, maybe she stayed for us then. Who knows? You'd have to ask her."

"Do you have any idea who his most recent affair was?"

Haley laughed. "Anyone within a one-hundred-mile radius between twenty-two and fifty. Take your pick." She gave me a sudden, curious look. "I'm surprised he didn't hit on you."

I opened my mouth and closed it again. "You don't really think he had affairs with that many women, do you?"

"Just ask the women at his firm," she said. "He's probably messed around with everyone of them."

"How did you find out about this?"

Haley turned her head and flicked her ashes into a small silver ashtray. "I walked in on him, once," she said, almost inaudibly. "Then I started asking around," she added as she looked back at me. "You'd be amazed at what people will tell you if you just ask."

I laughed, and she looked annoyed. "Sorry," I said. "I didn't mean to laugh, but I know just what you mean. Who was it you talked to? Would you mind telling me?''

"Anna Schulz told me the most stuff. She was my dad's secretary. If you tell her I told you that, she'd kill me though, so don't tell, okay?''

"I won't," I said. "Did you talk to anyone else about it?''

"Well, I think my Aunt Audrey and my Aunt Sue know, and Uncle Gerry, but they never said anything to me about it. Don't want to traumatize the kid, right?''

I gave her a lopsided smile, and nodded. "Did you talk to anyone else at the firm?''

"No. I tried talking to Sharon Falk but she wouldn't say anything.''

"Who was the woman you caught him with?''

"Some secretary. She doesn't work there anymore.''

"Do you know her name?''

Haley shook her head.

"Do you have any other ideas?" I said. "Anyone he was fighting with, having trouble with, anything like that?''

Haley thought for a few moments. "You mean unusual fights, or just regular, everyday?''

"Either," I said.

"Well, he and my mom fought a lot but that's just normal and I know *she* didn't do it. Paul and my dad never got along too well, but that was just normal stuff, too. I don't know about any real fights he ever had with anybody, like big arguments or anything.''

"Okay," I said. "Thanks, Haley. You've actually

been a big help. You told me more than anyone else has, so far.''

She smiled and looked proud of herself. ''Well, if I think of anything else, I'll let you know, okay?''

''Okay,'' I said with a smile. ''I'll talk to you later.''

When I walked downstairs, I called Olivia's name but she didn't answer, so I let myself out the front door.

''Did you learn anything from Haley?'' Emily asked when I walked into the library. Janice didn't say anything, but she gave me an expectant look.

''Yeah, I sure did,'' I said. ''She says Phillip was having affairs with every woman in town and Olivia knew all about it but she never said anything.''

''Why would she do that?'' Emily said.

''I don't know,'' I said with a shrug. ''Maybe they were both having affairs.''

Janice looked shocked and Emily smiled. ''My, my, how sophisticated,'' Emily said.

''She probably just stayed with him because of the kids,'' I said. ''Your own interests aren't always the first priority, you know.''

Janice nodded with a sad face and Emily looked at me like I was nuts.

''Well, at least you have your motive now,'' Emily said.

''For whom?'' I said.

''For Olivia.''

''I don't know,'' I said. ''Why would she kill him now if it had been going on for years and she knew about it all the time?''

"Maybe she really didn't know," Emily said. "Maybe Haley just thinks she knew."

I raised an eyebrow. "Well, that's true," I said.

Janice looked like she was thinking hard. "Or maybe," she said, "maybe she never cared all that much before because she thought the affairs didn't mean anything but she thought this one was different. Like more serious, or more of a threat?"

I nodded. "That's possible, too. Good thinking, you guys." Janice looked pleased and so did Emily, but Emily tried not to show it.

We went back and forth for about five more minutes with more, relatively unproductive speculation, and then got back to work. They both stayed late again because of the crunch, and we worked straight through to a quarter to seven. By that time we were all practically starving to death, so I took everyone out to Pizza Man (Janice's choice) on North Avenue. It was still about seventy-five degrees, so we sat outside, ordered a bottle of wine, and made a night of it.

THE NEXT DAY was Tuesday, July 15, the first time I met with Gerry. I woke up with a bit of a headache from the wine, but it was gone by the time I'd had breakfast. I finished my banana and mango by eight o'clock and went to work in the library with my second cup of tea before Janice and Emily even showed up. I still had the last big issue to complete and I had to get it done that day. The brief wasn't due until Friday, but I'd planned to have it done on Monday, and now I was a day behind schedule. I worked straight through the afternoon, not even bothering to break for lunch, and by a quarter after three, I was completely finished with the horrible brief. I ran upstairs, changed my clothes, and told everyone I'd see them later. It was time to go see Gerry.

Gerry's (and, formerly, Phillip's) firm is in an old three-story building on East Mason Street. I took the stairs to the second floor and walked into a small but nicely furnished lobby, with an Oriental rug, a dark walnut desk, a small couch, and two chairs upholstered in a blue and beige striped fabric. There were brass lamps on the tables and a young receptionist behind the desk.

"May I help you?" she said.

"I have an appointment with Gerard Barry," I said. "My name is Beth Hartley."

"What is this regarding?" she asked.

"It's a personal matter," I said with a smile. "He's expecting me."

A few moments later, Gerry appeared, wearing a wrinkled blue shirt, a striped tie, and a big grin. "Beth, come on back," he said. He touched my shoulder and guided me in the direction of his office. As we were about to enter, I saw Anna Schulz, Phillip's secretary, come out of another. She looked at me and quickly looked away.

Gerry's office was very conservative—a walnut desk and credenza, floor-to-ceiling bookcases, a brown leather couch. The wing chairs in front of the desk were dark green with a little paisley print, kind of like a tie. The couch was covered with papers, all neatly stacked in piles. Same for the chairs.

"Excuse the mess," he said, and removed the papers from one of the chairs. "Please, sit down."

"Thanks," I said. "I hope this isn't a bad time for you. You look like you're really busy."

He laughed. "We're always busy," he said "But this is important. I'd like to help in anyway I can. I want Phillip's killer caught. We all do."

I nodded and looked at him for a moment. "Well, I'll get right to the point then," I said. "Did Phillip have any enemies that you know of?"

Gerry frowned. "Well, enemy's a rather strong word," he said. "Certainly there were people who disliked him, but enemies…there's no one I would describe as an enemy."

"Who disliked him?" I said. "And why?"

"No one in particular," he said. "I only meant that we all have people who don't like us. Phillip was a very forceful person with strong opinions. When he disagreed with someone, he let them know it. Occasionally he'd knock someone's nose out of joint. That's all I meant."

"How about the people in the office? Did he get along with them?"

Gerry furrowed his brow. "Well, these people were Phillip's employees," he said. "They had to answer to him for everything they did. There's always something of a strain between people in those relative positions. It's unavoidable."

"How many people do you have working here?" I said.

"Four…well, three CPAs now, and four secretaries. Why do you ask?"

"I'd like to talk to them all, eventually, if that's all right."

"Certainly," Gerry said. "One of our accountants, Bob Hennison, is out of the country, though, so you'll have to wait a while to talk to him. And his secretary's on vacation until he gets back."

"Do you know when he'll be back?" I said.

"I'm not sure," Gerry said. "Sometime in the next week or two, I believe."

"Does he know about Phillip's death?"

"Yes, he's been informed."

I nodded. "Okay. Well, what about you?" I said. "Did you find it easy to work with Phillip?"

"Yes, of course I found it easy to work with him," he said with a hint of annoyance. "He was my brother."

I gave him a vague smile. "The whole business is yours, now, isn't it?" I said.

Now he gave me a look of downright irritation. "We have a shareholders' agreement," he said. "I buy his shares. I pay big money to his estate. I don't come out ahead. Not exactly a motive for murder, now is it?"

"I was just asking," I said. My next question was sure to annoy him even more but at that point I figured I had nothing to lose so I just blurted it out. "Can you tell me anything about the affairs he was having?"

Gerry sat upright and his face turned a bit red. "Who told you that?" he said.

I took a deep breath. "I promised not to tell."

He set his jaw and glared at me.

"I'm sorry," I said. "I know it's none of my business, but he's been murdered and I'm trying to find out who did it. The more I know about his life and the people in it, the more likely I'll be able to find the answer. That's how I did it the last time."

One corner of his mouth turned up just a little. "The Marquette student," he said.

I nodded. "I know I'm not very experienced at this, but I figure if something works once, it makes sense to do it that way again."

Gerry leaned back in his chair and studied my face. Then he let out a deep breath and relaxed his shoulders. "Well, I guess you have a point," he said. "I'm sorry I got my feathers ruffled. I guess I forgot why you were asking. Go ahead, what would you like to know?"

"I'd like to know the names of the women he had affairs with, if that's possible," I said.

Gerry gave me a funny look, removed his glasses, and rubbed his eyes. "I'll have to make you a list," he said. "It may take some time."

"You're kidding?" I said.

He raised his eyebrows. "I'm afraid not," he said. "Of course, I don't know who all of them were."

I tried to keep my reaction to myself. "How about his clients?" I asked. "Do you think there could be anything there?"

"Affairs, you mean?"

"No, I meant suspects, possible motives. Why? You don't think he was having affairs with his clients, too, do you?"

He gave me a look that said "Why not?"

"I was thinking maybe he got involved in something with a client," I said, "or he found something out about someone and they wanted to keep him quiet."

Gerry wrinkled his brow. "I think you're letting your imagination runaway with you," he said.

"Well, you never know. Peter said he'd been working on something pretty big in the last couple of months and he was always working nights and weekends."

Gerry gave me a solicitous smile. "We have a lot of big accounts," he said. "Clients who bring us all of their financial work. There's nothing out of the ordinary about it."

"Was he working on something major when he died?"

"He may have been," Gerry said. "I really don't know."

I nodded. I hesitated a little before asking the next question. "Do you think Olivia knew about Phillip's affairs?"

Gerry raised his eyebrows. "I really don't see how she couldn't have," he said.

"How long do you think she knew?"

"For years, I'm sure. Why? What are you driving at?"

"Well, nothing, really," I said with a shrug. "It's just that…"

"If you're thinking Olivia killed Phillip because he was involved with another woman," Gerry said, "you're surely wrong. That business had gone on far too long for her to suddenly become so angry that she'd kill him." He shook his head. "She's not the type, anyway."

"Okay," I said. "Is there anyone else *you* think I should talk to? Anyone who might know something?"

Gerry tilted his head and thought for a moment. "There is someone I'd like you to talk to as soon as possible," he said. "Sharon Falk. She's one of our CPAs and she's been going through Phillip's files for me to get things in order. I don't expect she'll find anything such as you have in mind, but I can ask her to keep an eye out for anything suspicious."

Gerry pressed a button on his phone, waited a few moments, and pressed another. "Where's Ms. Falk?" he said into the speaker.

"She's at Thorgood & Marshall, Mr. Barry," a woman's voice answered. "I don't expect her back today. Is it urgent?"

"No, never mind," Gerry said.

"I'll see that she gets in touch with you," he said as he walked toward the door.

"Thanks," I said, and I stood to follow him. "You'll let me know when you've finished the list?"

"Yes, I will," he said.

"Oh, I just thought of something else," I said. "I wanted to ask you about Paul."

Gerry gave me a puzzled look. "What about Paul?"

"Was he going to join the firm after he graduated?"

"That was my understanding," Gerry said.

"Will he still be joining, now that Phillip is gone?"

"I don't believe so," he said.

"SOMEONE NAMED Anna Schulz called while you were out," Janice said when I got home. "She sounded like it was really important. She wants you to call her at home tonight, not at the office."

I frowned. "That's weird. She was Phillip's secretary. I just saw her at their office. I wonder why she didn't say anything then."

"Well, she obviously doesn't want anyone to know she's talking to you," Emily said.

"Yes," I said. "But why?"

She gave me a snide little smile. "Ooh, intrigue, mystery, suspense."

I gave her a dirty look.

It was already four-thirty, and Janice and Emily left at six. I had some raspberry yogurt and a banana for supper, and called Anna Schulz as soon as I was done.

Even her "hello" sounded nervous.

"Is this Anna Schulz?" I said.

"Yes," she said in an almost panicky voice.

"This is Beth Hartley," I said, "returning your call. Are you all right?"

"I need to talk to you," she said. "But not on the phone."

"Would you like me to come there? Or do you want to come to my house?"

"No, no," she said. "It has to be somewhere else. Can I meet you somewhere?"

"Sure," I said. "You mean like a restaurant?"

"Yes, yes, that would be good," she said. "There's a restaurant called Omega on Twenty-seventh Street near the Southgate shopping center. Can you meet me there for breakfast tomorrow morning? It would have to be very early.''

"Sure," I said. "What time?"

"Seven o'clock?"

"Okay," I said. "Seven o'clock is fine. I'll see you then. And thanks, Anna."

I penciled in the appointment on my calendar and frowned. Either Anna Schulz had something extremely important to tell me, or she was too melodramatic for words. I NordicTracked for thirty minutes to dissipate some of my nervous energy, read for a while, and was just about to go to bed when she called me back. She changed our breakfast appointment from seven to nine. She had something very important she had to do first.

SIX

I was at the restaurant the next morning at a quarter to nine, and I requested a table with a view of the door so I'd be sure not to miss Anna when she came in. I ordered coffee and waited. And waited and waited and waited. Anna never showed up.

At ten, I called her apartment from a pay phone, but got no answer. I called again when I got home, but still there was no answer. I guessed that she had gone to the office by now, but I didn't want to call her there since she'd seemed so concerned that our meeting be kept secret. I'd just have to wait to hear from her.

"Where were you?" Emily said when I walked into the library. Janice looked up and waited for me to answer.

"I was supposed to meet Phillip's secretary for breakfast, but she never showed up."

Emily frowned. "Isn't that the one who called yesterday?"

"Yeah, and I called her house but she doesn't answer."

"Maybe she's at work," Janice said.

"Yeah, maybe. But I don't want to call there because she doesn't want anyone to know she's talking to me."

"You want me to call for you?" Janice said.

I raised my eyebrows and considered it for a moment. "No," I said. "I think I'll just wait for her to call me."

Well, I waited the rest of the afternoon, expecting her to call any minute, but she never did.

At five-thirty, after everyone had gone home, Brian called.

"Beth," he said, in a really cool voice, "I have something I need to talk to you about but I'd like to do it in person. Can I stop by in a little while?"

"Sure," I said, trying to keep the distress out of my voice. "What time?"

"Half an hour."

"Okay," I said. "I'll see you then. Brian?"

"I'll talk to you later, Beth."

"ANNA SCHULZ," Brian said as soon as I let him in. Then he watched my face for a reaction.

I opened my eyes wide and stared at him.

"Are you acquainted with her?" he said.

"Yes," I said. "She was Phillip's secretary. Why? What do you know about her?"

"Not much," Brian said, "except that she was found murdered this morning in Phillip Barry's office. And, she had a note in her pocket with your name and phone number on it."

"Oh, my gosh," I said. "Brian, I was supposed to have breakfast with her this morning but she never showed up. She said she really wanted to talk to me but she didn't want to do it on the phone."

"Did she say what it was about?"

"No, but I assumed it was about Phillip's death. She sounded like it was really important."

"Where and when?" Brian said.

"Where and when what?"

"Where and when were you supposed to meet her?" he said.

"Oh. At the Omega Restaurant on Twenty-seventh Street, at nine o'clock. At first she wanted to meet at seven, but then she called back and changed it to nine because she had to do something first."

"Did she say what?"

"No, but she said it was very important."

"Okay," Brian said, and nodded his head. He put his I'm-a-detective-and-I'm-busy-thinking-detective-thoughts look on his face, so I waited until he was done.

"How well did you know her?" he said.

"I didn't know her at all," I said. "I only met her at the wake, and the only other time I talked to her was on the phone yesterday."

I found it absolutely amazing, but he looked as if he didn't believe me.

"Have you ever been to her apartment?" he asked then.

I gaped at him. "No!" I said. "I just told you. I didn't even know her."

Brian nodded and watched my face. "I'm going to her place now. Maybe you'd like to come with me."

I frowned and stared at him for a moment. "Why would you want me to go with you?" I said.

He shrugged. "I'm sure you'd end up snooping around there sooner or later. This way I can keep an eye on you while you're doing it. And hey, who knows? Maybe you'll notice something that I would've missed. You *are* Miss Supersleuth, aren't you?''

My face got hot and I could feel tears welling up, but I fought to keep from crying. I didn't say anything, because I knew my voice would shake.

"Let's go," Brian said. "You're coming with me."

I grabbed my purse and followed him without a word, still afraid my voice would break if I spoke. I calmed down sufficiently on the way there to enable me to at least *act* as if everything was normal, but I kept pretty quiet, just the same.

Anna's flat was off Howell Avenue, on the south side of Milwaukee, in a quiet neighborhood with tree-lined streets. The house was a typical frame house with aluminum siding and a front porch. It was a duplex, and Anna lived upstairs. Brian rang the downstairs bell, spoke to the owner for a few moments, and we walked on up.

As we approached the top of the stairs, I could hear some tiny feet slide across the flooring and scratch at the door. We opened the door to a little French poodle, all white, except some of its fur had brown edges. He was a casual sort of dog—no big bows or fancy shaved patches. He seemed almost disappointed when he saw us, but his tail wagged happily just the same.

"I wonder if anyone's fed this poor little thing," I said. "Don't the people downstairs know about him?''

"I'm sure they do," Brian said. "What they don't know yet is that Anna Schulz is dead."

"Oh," I said. "Oh, gosh. Let me see if I can find him something to eat." Brian nodded and started looking around. "Don't do anything without me," I said as he left the room. He gave me a really irritated look but didn't reply.

I found some dog food under the sink, filled his bowl, and filled another one with cool water. He jumped and skittered across the floor as I was giving him the food, and then he gobbled it all up like he hadn't eaten in days. Poor little guy. He didn't know it yet, but his favorite friend was never coming back.

I found Brian in the living room, looking through an old rolltop desk. The place looked like Anna Schulz. I'd only seen her twice, but I could see she was sort of an old-world type. She was in her late thirties, about five-five or -six, a rather large woman maybe twenty pounds overweight. Her hair was a dark blond, obviously undyed, and she wore it in a bun at the nape of her neck. Her clothing was very conservative and plain. When I saw her at Phillip's office the day I went to see Gerry, she was wearing a blue cotton skirt, a white blouse, and a plain blue cardigan draped over her shoulders.

Anna's living room was carpeted in olive green, a sort of fuzzy rug with a squiggly design in it. She had a couch upholstered in worn gold brocade, with an orange and white crocheted afghan folded neatly across the top. The one chair in the room, other than the desk chair, was a rust-colored recliner. Next to the chair was a little table. There was nothing on it but a

Bible with a ribbon keeping the place where she'd last been reading. At the foot of the chair was a small cushion with the name "Scamper" embroidered on the plaid fabric.

The walls were covered with framed cross-stitch work—*Bless This Home,* read one; another was an alphabet and number sampler; the rest, pictures of famous places. Everything was very homey and very neat. The kitchen had been spotless, too.

There were two tables against the wall under the lace-curtained windows facing the street. They looked like sofa tables made of mission oak. Each one was covered with framed photographs. One was of an old woman and an old man in a formal, unsmiling pose. Another showed a younger Anna, maybe fourteen or fifteen, with another girl who looked so much like Anna she could only have been her sister. They had their arms around each other and were smiling happily. I sighed and turned away.

"Did you find anything?" I asked Brian.

"Nothing yet," he said. He was carefully lifting papers from the desk by their very edges. I love it when he does that.

I started to walk toward the back of the house. "Hey, don't touch anything," Brian said. "Just look."

I gave him an injured look and huffed away. Off a hallway connected to the living room were a bathroom, Anna's bedroom, and another room which I assumed was a second bedroom, though I couldn't be sure since the door was closed. I knew if I opened it,

Brian would've had a fit, so I went past it and into Anna's bedroom, instead.

The room was small, painted off-white, with no pictures on the walls. The closet was open so I peered inside and saw half a dozen skirts, four blouses, and two dresses on metal hangers. On the floor, three pairs of sturdy shoes were lined up in a row. No shelves. The drawers of her oak dresser (I opened them *very quietly*) contained folded underwear, stockings, a few sweaters, and several pairs of slacks. Each drawer contained a little sachet, all handmade from the look of them. The scent was really pretty—roses, I think. The mirror behind the dresser was tiny, the kind meant for a foyer or hallway. It was the only mirror in the room. On the top of the dresser was an off-white crocheted runner. There was a jewelry box with a string of pearls (they looked old), matching drop earrings, and a brooch studded with tiny pearls and amethysts.

A white gauze nightgown was folded and placed on top of the pillow of her twin-size bed. The bedspread was chenille, just like the one I'd had when I was little, only hers was beige and mine had been a light pink.

The bathroom across the hall was clean, like everything else, and painted a light glossy green. There was a bathtub but no shower curtain, although there was a shower head. A washcloth hung over the faucet, dry and stiff. The one thing that surprised me was that her towels were a thick, plush green, with her initials monogrammed at the bottom. Somehow, that didn't fit with everything else.

I went back to the living room where I found Brian petting the dog.

"That's a boy," he was saying, as he scratched behind the dog's ears.

I smiled. "I think his name is Scamper," I said. As soon as I said his name, Scamper's ears twitched and he padded over to me, his tail wagging away.

"Hey, Scamper," I said, as I reached down to pet his warm head. "What are we going to do with you?"

Brian was about to say something when I cut him off. "Well, we can't just leave him here," I said. "He'd starve to death. Besides, he needs love and affection."

"You don't even like dogs," Brian said with an exasperated look.

"I know," I said. "I don't usually, but I like this one. Look at his sweet little face. We can't just leave him here."

Brian shook his head and let out a sigh. "All right, take him home with you for now. You can take care of him until we figure out what to do with him."

I grinned happily and I could swear, so did Scamper.

"Come on, boy," Brian said. "Let's go to Auntie Beth's house."

"You mean you're done already?" I said. I should've tried to keep the reproach out of my voice.

Brian glowered at me. "No, I'm not done," he said. "We'll go over the place very thoroughly tomorrow. I just wanted to get a sneak preview."

"Didn't you find anything in the desk?" I asked.

Brian hesitated just a bit. "No," he said. "I didn't."

Yeah, sure, Brian. Well, I'd be back tonight to see for myself.

We informed the man downstairs (named Mr. Royce) that we were taking Anna's dog. Brian told Mr. Royce about Anna's death and asked him not to disturb anything until he had their "okay." Then he dropped me off with Scamper and left me to deal with him myself, just as I was hoping he would. I made myself some supper, took the dog for a walk to do you-know-what, and read until about nine-fifteen.

Then I went back to Anna's place.

SEVEN

I KNOCKED ON Mr. Royce's door, praying that he'd be home, and he was. He peered out and squinted a little before a look of recognition brightened his face. "Oh, hello, Miss," he said. "I didn't know it was you at first."

"Hi, Mr. Royce," I said with my most innocent smile. "I just came back to get some more things for Scamper. I forgot his dog food and his bed."

"Well, we certainly can't have that now, can we? Hang on just a minute and I'll walk you up."

"Oh, don't bother," I said quickly. "I might be a while, anyway. I want to look around and make sure I'm not forgetting anything else."

He studied my face for a moment and shrugged. "Suit yourself, Miss. Just leave the keys under the doormat when you're finished. I'm turning in."

"Okay, I will," I said. "Thanks a lot, Mr. Royce."

I looked around to see that no one was watching (why, I don't know), and let myself in. The exterior door to Anna's flat was to the left of Mr. Royce's door, and the steps were inside. The interior door required a second key, which Mr. Royce had given me. I unlocked the door and opened it as quietly as I could. I was sure there was no one else there, but for some reason, I was nervous. I willed myself to calm down, tiptoed into the living room, and looked around, trying to decide where to begin. I wanted to look through the desk, but I was even more anxious to see the second bedroom and the other closets.

I went for the closets first. There were only two, one in the living room and one in the hallway near the bathroom. I guessed the hallway one to be a linen closet and I was right. It had four shelves. Two of them held neatly folded, plain white towels and wash-cloths and some more of the plush green mono-grammed ones; the other two, neatly folded and *ironed,* plain white sheets and pillowcases. I closed the door.

The living room closet was a coat closet, with six heavy coat hangers, a hatbox on a shelf, and a pair of boots on the floor. Three of the hangers held a beige raincoat, an olive green wool winter coat in a plastic protector, and a lightweight jacket made of brown cotton. I checked the pockets, but they were all empty.

The hatbox was up high and was hard to reach, so I used one of the hangers to pull it down. I opened it, expecting to find hats, but it was filled to the top with old photographs. I took them out, one at a time, and carefully studied each one. Most of them were of the same people I'd seen in the photographs on Anna's tables, some were of people I didn't recognize at all, and a few showed Gerry and Phillip in the office, Sharon Falk and Gerry in the office, Phillip, Sharon Falk, and a small child in the office, Phillip and Anna in the office, and so on. I looked through them all and put them back.

On to the mysterious bedroom. I opened the door,

turned on the light, and gasped. I couldn't believe what I was seeing. This must have been the room to which Anna went when she wanted to be someone else. There was nothing in there that even remotely resembled the rest of her flat. She had a very large-screened television, a stair-stepper, and a weight bench, with free weights all over the place. The ones on the bar totaled seventy pounds. The walls were mirrored—big floor-to-ceiling mirrors. All except the walls with the pictures, that is.

On that wall was a life-size blowup of Linda Hamilton wearing her *Terminator 2* muscles. Anna's idol? There were smaller pictures of other women, all with enviable bodies—Cheryl Ladd and Farrah Fawcett from the old ''Charlie's Angels'' days, that woman who plays Lois Lane on the new ''Superman'' show, and a bunch of others I couldn't identify.

And then there was Phillip Barry.

His picture was life-size, too. He had a startled look on his face, mixed with a bit of annoyance. I could see the picture was taken in his office, and he was wearing a business suit. He was also wearing a dart—right in the center of his forehead.

I sat down on the weight bench and ran this new information through my head. Had Anna been in love with Phillip? Did she think she could attract him if she exercised her way to a gorgeous body? Maybe she thought she could pin him to the ground with her enormous muscles. It was ridiculous. None of it made any sense.

Maybe she'd actually had an affair with him and he broke it off. Could *she* have killed him? On the other hand, if she did kill him, who killed her? I sat there for a while and stared at Phillip's picture while I mulled over the possibilities. I didn't have any great flashes of brilliance so I decided to let it go and search the desk.

I closed the door and went back to the living room. The desk was an oak rolltop, pretty scratched up, with some of the varnish peeling off. At the back were vertical slots where Anna had placed her mail and some other papers. I started from the left side and removed everything in the first slot. Nothing but charge card bills. I read through the purchases but nothing struck me as significant. Linens, bathing suits, jewelry, a purse. I put the bills back and removed the papers from the next slot. Here was a phone bill, an electric bill, and a rent receipt. The date on the phone bill was two weeks before Phillip's death. I looked through the list of calls. The local ones weren't listed, of course, and there was only one long-distance number. Anna had called that same number every Sunday night during the billing period and had always talked for approximately one hour. I copied the number on a sheet of stationery I found on the top of the desk and replaced the bills. What I really wanted to know was whom she'd called between Phillip's death and her own. Brian could certainly get ahold of information like that, but would he share it with me? Ha, not likely.

The next slot contained three letters from Anna's sister. She lived in Houston, Texas, the same place to which the long distance phone calls were made. The letters were dated two weeks apart and it was just about time for the next one, if that was her habit. I read each one but none contained any reference to Phillip Barry, nor anything else I deemed significant. I copied the address and put them back.

The next slot was filled with grocery-store coupons, the one after that, a booklet with coupons for making car payments. The others were empty.

The surface of the desk was neat and relatively clear. It had a blotter with worn, tan leather edges, a scissors and a letter opener, the stationery, and a pencil holder. That was it.

There was only one drawer, right in the center. It stuck when I tried to open it, but after a few careful yanks, I was successful. It held paper clips (lined up in neat little rows), a small stapler, a box of staples, a ruler, several pens, a pad of paper, and some more stationery. I checked to see if the drawer had a false bottom (if you've read about my investigation of Dave Grezinski's murder, you'll know why I did *that*), and closed the drawer. No false bottom, by the way.

I got up from the desk and looked around the room to see if there was anything I'd missed. I hadn't, as far as I could see, and it was time I got out of there anyway. I took Scamper's bed and all the dog food I could find, locked up, put the keys under Mr. Royce's mat, and went home.

"HEY, WHERE'D YOU GET the puppy?" Janice said when she came in the next day. "Here, boy," she said to Scamper. "What's your name?" Scamper padded right over to Janice, tail wagging happily, and gave her a doggy kiss on the hand.

I laughed. "His name is Scamper," I said. "He belonged to Anna Schulz, Phillip's secretary."

Janice frowned. "What do you mean, belonged? Why do you have him?" I could see from her face that she already suspected what my answer would be.

"Anna Schulz was found murdered yesterday, in Phillip's office," I said. "She was shot."

"Oh, no," Janice said. She gave Scamper a sad look and lowered herself to a chair.

"Brian and I went over to her place yesterday, and Scamper was there, all by himself. He hadn't been fed and he obviously had no one to take care of him, so I took him home."

"Are you going to keep him?"

"I doubt it," I said. "I don't really want to have to take care of a dog, and Anna has a sister in Houston, anyway. She'll probably want him."

"Yeah," Janice said. She scratched Scamper behind the ears and sighed. "Do they have any idea who killed her?" she asked.

"No, but they think it might be the same person who killed Phillip. It looks like it could be the same gun."

"Wow," Janice said, and then scrunched up her face. "You'd better be careful."

I smiled. "Don't worry, I will."

"Hey, where'd you get the mutt?" Emily said as she walked past him toward the coffeepot.

"He's not a mutt, he's a French poodle," I said.

"You're kidding?" she said with a look of distaste. "He sure doesn't look like a French poodle."

"Well, he is."

"What's he doing here?" she said. Scamper took one look at Emily and left the room. Janice said, "I'd better get to work," and went after him.

I told Emily the same story I told Janice.

"So, Brian's talking to you again, huh?" I couldn't be sure, but I could swear she almost looked disappointed. You have to understand something about Emily. She and Brian have a "history" and I'm not sure she's over it yet. She's married to someone else (Phil), who loves her to death despite the fact that she treats him like dirt half the time. She and Brian met through her brother (who's also a cop), and they went out for a while before she went to law school. But then he went back to his wife, whom he'd divorced a year earlier, to try to work things out. They never did, of course, but by then Emily had already met Phil. I think she really wishes sometimes that she had Brian back, so that's why she acts a little weird where Brian and I are concerned.

"Well, he's talking to me," I said, "but I think he's still upset." That ought to make her feel better.

"He'll get over it," she said.

We worked all morning long, with no interruptions, and broke for lunch at twelve-thirty. We were still in the middle of our nacho and taco feast when Brian came to the door.

He gave Emily and Janice polite nods (really unfriendly, for him) and asked to speak to me privately. Great. Now what?

"We can go in the library," I said.

Brian followed me in without a word. When I'd closed the library doors, he gave me a very hard look.

"You wouldn't believe what we found in Anna Schulz's flat," Brian said. He watched for my response, with no expression on his face.

"Really?" I said. "What did you find?"

"Funny thing, though," he said, ignoring my question, "there were a few things we *didn't* find—things that were there yesterday when you and I were there. The dog's cushion was missing from the living room and so was the dog food we left under the sink. What do you think could've happened to them, Beth?"

I shrugged and tried to look cool, but my face got all red and that really messed up the effect. I rolled my eyes and sighed. "All I did was go back to get his dog food," I said, "and then I remembered the cushion so I took that, too. I thought maybe he used it to sleep on and he did. I put it right next to my bed and he slept on it all night. What's so wrong with that?"

Brian didn't alter his expression one single bit.

"Brian," I said, "why are you so upset? I didn't do anything. I didn't take anything else and I didn't touch anything. What are you so upset about?"

"Forget it," he said. "Just drop it."

"So, what did you find?" I said. "Aren't you going to tell me?"

He looked down at the floor and tightened his jaw. "Nothing you don't already know about," he said. And he left. Again.

I WAS IN THE LIBRARY, working, when I got an almost frantic call from Gerry.

"You've heard about Anna," he said, more as a statement than a question.

"Yes," I said. "I did. I'm so sorry, Gerry."

"I understand you were going to meet with her. What's going on here? First she talks to you and then she's found murdered? What did she say to you?"

I stood for a while with my mouth open, not knowing what to say. "Well, nothing," I finally said. "She didn't say anything to me. She said she didn't want to talk on the phone and I had to meet her somewhere but when I went to meet her she never showed up and then I found out she was dead. You don't think *I* had anything to do with it, do you?"

"All I know is, one minute she's talking to you and the next minute she's dead. You put it together."

I took a deep breath and let it out. "Gerry," I said, "no one could even have known she was talking to me, she was so secretive about it." I stopped. "Wait a minute. How did you know I was going to talk to her? Did she tell you that?"

"No, my secretary told me."

"When did she tell you?"

"This morning. Why? What difference does it make?"

"I don't know," I said. "None, I guess. I'm just surprised Anna told her, that's all."

"Well, I think it might be best if you stayed out of this from now on," Gerry said.

"I can't do that," I said. "I made a promise to Peter and I'm going to keep it. If you think my involvement somehow caused Anna's death, you're crazy. That's just ridiculous. She changed our appointment to a later time because she said she had something she had to do first. My guess is that she knew who the killer was, which is what she was going to tell me, and she decided at the last minute to confront him first and that's probably what got her killed.''

Gerry was silent for a few moments. "Oh, Lord," he finally said. "You may be right."

Yeah, no kidding, Sherlock.

"All right. Well, why don't you come by the office when you have a chance," he said. "I have that information you asked for."

"Are you free now?"

"Uh...sure," he said.

"I'll be right there."

WHEN I ARRIVED, the receptionist told me to walk on back. Gerry was waiting for me.

He handed me the list without even saying hello. "I can't give you their addresses," he said. "And this is between the two of us. I don't want anyone to know I gave you this information."

I nodded. "Don't worry," I said. "I won't tell anyone." I opened the folded sheet of paper, read it, and looked up. "There are only three names on here. I thought you said there was a whole bunch of them."

"Those were the only names I could remember," he said.

"Were they employees of your firm?"

Gerry hesitated, gave me a strange look, and said, "Phillip had a thing for secretaries."

I watched his face for a bit, but he wasn't giving anything away. I didn't believe for a moment that he'd given me a complete list of those he remembered. He looked a mess. His hair was sticking up, like he'd been running his hands through it, and he had rings of sweat under his arms. It wasn't all that warm.

He let out a nervous laugh for no apparent reason. "I want to know what's going on here," he said. "What was Anna doing here so early and how did her killer get in the building?"

"She probably let him in," I said. "Maybe she knew who Phillip's killer was and even why he killed him, and she arranged to meet him here for some reason."

Gerry shook his head and frowned. "But why would anyone be stupid enough to arrange to meet someone they knew was a murderer, and in a deserted building of all places?"

I raised my eyebrows and shrugged. "I don't know," I said, "but it's certainly been done before. Maybe she was blackmailing the person and he'd already paid her some money, so she just didn't think he'd kill her. I know it's incredibly stupid, but it is plausible."

He shook his head again. "But why would she meet the killer here? And how would she know who killed Phillip?"

"I don't know," I said. "Maybe it has something to do with the firm." Gerry shot me an angry look.

"What I mean is, maybe it has to do with a client or even one of your employees. It is possible, you know."

Gerry leaned forward and put his head in his hands. He looked up after a bit, and stared at me. "I'd like you to talk to my secretary," he said. "I think she may know more than she's telling me."

"Does she know you want me to talk to her?" I asked.

"She will in a moment." He pushed a button on his telephone and said, "Would you come in here, please," to whomever picked up on the other end.

EIGHT

A FEW MOMENTS LATER, a young woman I'd seen at Phillip's funeral entered the room. She looked no more than twenty, thin and petite, with long, light-brown hair worn loose except for the front portion which was pulled back from her face with a barrette. She looked at me and stiffened. "Yes?" she said to Gerry, and gave him a questioning look.

He introduced us (her name was Joanne Donnelly) and essentially ordered her to talk to me. "And be cooperative," he added.

She looked confused and a little frightened but it subsided a bit when he gave her a reassuring smile. "I'll be in Phillip's office," he told her, and he closed the door behind him.

"You think Anna got killed because of me, don't you?" I said.

Joanne looked close to tears and nodded her head.

"She didn't," I said. "She really didn't. I think she was killed because she knew who killed Phillip and she arranged to meet him here, probably to blackmail him or something. She never even got to talk to me, although I think she was going to tell me who did it."

"See," Joanne said in a shaky voice. "They could've killed her to keep her from telling you."

"I can see why you might think that," I said. "But

I'm sure it's not true. It just doesn't make sense. If she was killed because she knew something, she would've been killed anyway, even if she hadn't intended to tell me.''

I was convinced, but Joanne looked confused.

"No one knows you're talking to me," I said, "except for Mr. Barry. You have nothing to worry about, and if you do know something, it might help us find out who killed Anna.''

Now she started to cry. "I don't know anything,'' she said. "I don't know who did it.'' She sat down on the edge of the couch and wiped her nose with a tissue she took from her pocket.

"What did Anna say to you?'' I said. "Mr. Barry said she told you she was going to talk to me. Did she tell you why she wanted to talk to me?''

Joanne nodded and wiped a tear from her cheek. "She said she wanted to talk to you about Mr. Barry's murder.''

"That's all she said? She didn't say anything else?''

Joanne shook her head.

"Can you remember when she told you that?''

"The other time you were here. She whispered it to me when you were leaving.''

"Was that the only time she said anything to you about Phillip's death?''

Joanne frowned. "Well, not exactly,'' she said.

"Can you remember what else she said? Even if it doesn't seem important to you, just anything she said.''

"Well, she was worried about her job. She said she

didn't know if she'd still have one now that Mr. Barry was gone.''

"Did she ever find out about that?"

"Yes, she said Mr. Barry said she could stay because they'd be replacing the other Mr. Barry someday anyway.''

I raised my eyebrows. "Do you know who they're going to replace him with?"

Joanne shrugged. "Another accountant, I guess."

"Joanne, do you have any idea at all what Anna could have known?"

She gave me a helpless look. "I really don't," she said. "I'm sorry."

"That's okay," I said with a smile. "Did you know Anna very well? Were you good friends?"

"No, not really," she said. "I've only been working here for two years and she was a lot older than me. I never saw her outside of work or anything."

"Did she ever mention her family?"

Joanne thought for a moment. "She talked about her sister sometimes. They were really close, I think. She always used her vacation time to visit her."

"What about friends?" I said. "Did she ever mention any?"

"No, not that I remember."

I sighed and stared out the window for a moment. Then I looked back at Joanne. "Did Anna ever say anything to you about Phillip having any kind of trouble with one of his clients?"

"You mean like someone giving him a hard time or something?"

"Yeah."

"I don't think so," she said with a frown.

"Have you ever heard anyone say anything about a client threatening someone or engaging in anything illegal, anything like that?"

"No," she said as she shook her head. "You mean you think one of the clients might've done it?"

"Well, it's just an idea," I said. "If Phillip had discovered some sort of illegal activity on the part of a client and the client was desperate to cover it up, he might've killed him to keep it quiet, and Anna might know about something like that since she was Phillip's secretary."

Joanne stared at me. "Wow," she said. "I see what you mean."

"Well, if you do think of something you've forgotten or if you just happen to hear something, would you let me know?"

She gave me an uncertain look.

"I'll give you my number," I said, "and you can wait until you get home from work to call me. That way you don't have to worry that someone will overhear you."

She smiled. "Okay," she said. "I will." Her smile changed to one of apology. "I'm sorry I thought it was your fault," she added.

"That's okay," I said.

"And I promise I'll help you in anyway I can, okay?"

"Well, I know Anna would appreciate that very much," I said. "And Mr. Barry, too. *Both* Mr. Barrys."

She smiled again and looked like she felt better. I

wrote my number on a small scrap of paper and told her to put it in her pocket. That way, even her boss wouldn't know she had it.

I walked out of Gerry's office with her and poked my head into Phillip's before I left, but Gerry wasn't there. Joanne looked around for him but couldn't find him, so I told her to tell him to give me a call if he wanted to talk any further.

WHEN I GOT HOME, I put Scamper out in the yard (it's fenced) to do all those things that dogs do, and then got out my phone book. Just my luck. Not one of the three names Gerry had given me were listed. I called information next, and got the number for Patricia Morgan. Miriam Beechman's was unpublished, however, and there was no number at all for Sandra Goldberg.

I dialed Patricia Morgan's number. No answer and no machine. I put the phone book away and joined Janice and Em in the library.

Emily gave me a weird look. "What have you been up to?" she said.

"Oh, I just went to talk to Gerry Barry again. He actually gave me a list of women Phillip had affairs with."

"A list?" she said with a laugh. "How many are there?"

"Only three," I said. "I was kind of disappointed."

Now Janice gave me the weird look.

"Well, I was just hoping I'd have a bunch of people to talk to. I was expecting more and all I got was three, and on top of that, I can't even get the phone numbers for two of them. How am I supposed to find these people?"

"Try the real estate records," Emily said.

I wrinkled my brow. "The real estate records? What do you mean?"

She gave me her Oh - it's - so - hard - to - be - patient - with - those - of - inferior - intelligence - but - I - guess - it's - my - lot - in - life look and said, "Go to the county courthouse and look in the Register of Deeds office. All you need is a name and you can find out where they live. Assuming they own property in Milwaukee County, of course, and assuming it's in their name and not just their husband's."

"Well, that's a lot of assumptions," I said. "But it's worth a shot," I added when she glowered at me. I looked at my watch. Two-thirty. Should I stay home and work like a good little ghostwriter or run on down to the Register of Deeds and take a quick look through the property files?

I let Scamper back in, told everyone I'd be back later, and headed for the Register of Deeds.

The Milwaukee County Courthouse is on Ninth and State, an impressive structure at least seven hundred feet wide, with Corinthian columns all around. The barrel-vaulted ceilings are twenty feet high and the hallways are made of marble. I went downstairs to the deed files and looked for Sandra Goldberg's name first, with no success. I checked Miriam Beechman next, not really expecting to find it, but I was in luck. She owned a house, in both her and her husband's names, on Brown Deer Road. From the address, I guessed it was pretty near Mayfair, one of our shopping malls. I let out a little yelp of glee (very unlawyer-like) and got a few disapproving stares.

Well, that took care of two out of three. The elusive Sandra Goldberg would have to wait. Maybe Patricia Morgan or Miriam Beechman would know who she was.

It was already three-thirty when I got home and I'd barely gotten any work done that day. I put Scamper back out in the yard and worked along with Janice and Emily until they left at five-fifteen. I fed Scamper, had a cold pasta salad I make with fettucini, about five different vegetables, Italian dressing, and parmesan cheese, and then brought my work to the kitchen for my usual evening stint. I could smell the grass, newly mown by my lawn service, mixed with the scent of pink and white roses, through my open window. A tiny bird was in my maple tree, singing his little heart out. A dog barked in the distance and a woodpecker chipped away at my neighbor's tree. A soft breeze caressed my face. I *couldn't* stand it anymore. I left my work on the table, called to Scamper, and took him out in the backyard. I let him run free while I stretched out in my hammock, closed my eyes, and breathed in the summer scents and listened to the summer sounds. I felt the warm sun on my skin, the air moving through my hair, and reveled in every little sensation. There's something about being outside in the middle of a sunny summer day that makes me feel as if the movement of time has slowed almost to a standstill. I feel, on those days, like I'm going to live for a very long time.

I WOKE UP Friday morning with a cold, wet nose in my face. I nearly died of fright until I realized it was Scamper.

"Hey, fuzzy," I said. "You want to go outside?"

He panted and pranced and jumped around, which I took to be a "yes" in dog language, so I let him out in the yard, took a quick shower, and let him in again after I got dressed.

"Well, what'll it be?" I said. "Hearty Beef Stew, or this really slimy, yucky stuff?"

He chose Hearty Beef Stew, smart dog. I put it in his bowl, filled his water dish, and made myself some rye toast and a cup of tea. Scamper finished his breakfast and lay down in the box I'd put near the back door. Two seconds later, he was fast asleep.

Half an hour later, Emily and Mrs. Gunther arrived.

"I hope you're going to keep out of my way today," Mrs. Gunther said to Scamper as she poured herself a cup of coffee. I gave her a look but she walked away without another word. Emily wrinkled her nose at him. "When was the last time you gave him a bath?" she said.

"A bath? I never gave him a bath. I figured Anna's sister could do that."

"You have got to be kidding. I really don't think you can afford to wait that long. He's starting to reek. Why don't you just take him to Cappoochino's?"

"What's that?" I said.

"It's a really cool dog-grooming place on Moorland and National. They even have a coffee bar."

I raised my eyebrows. "Well, I'll think about it," I said. She flashed me an annoyed look. "Fine, but in the meantime, the least you can do is keep him outside. It's disgusting to have a dirty dog right in your kitchen.''

I gave Scamper a consoling glance. ''You can stay here as long as you want to,'' I told him, and followed Emily to the library.

I got right down to work and finished the brief I was writing by ten-fifteen. Then I decided to call Anna's sister. I'd been putting it off, at first, because I was afraid of being the one to break the news of Anna's death, and later, because I just didn't know what to say. I really needed to talk to her before she left for Milwaukee, though, and Anna's wake was the next day. If she did want to take Scamper, she'd probably want to make some arrangements before she got here.

I brought my Phillip file to the kitchen, took a deep breath, and dialed the number.

''Hello?'' a woman said.

''Hello, my name is Beth Hartley,'' I said. ''I'm looking for the sister of Anna Schulz from Milwaukee. Do I have the right number?''

Silence.

''Hello?'' I said.

''Yes,'' the woman said. ''This is Margaret Furman. Anna Schulz was my sister. Who is calling, please?'' She had a slight German accent, but she sounded young, maybe early thirties.

''My name is Beth Hartley,'' I said again. ''I didn't know your sister well, but I'm a friend of the family of her boss, Phillip Barry.''

''Yes?'' she said.

"I'm calling, first of all, to tell you how sorry I am about Anna's death."

"Thank you," she said.

"And I wanted to let you know that I've been taking care of her dog."

"Yes, of course, Scamper. I was told he was being cared for by a friend."

"Would you like him, Mrs. Furman? He's a wonderful little dog and I'm sure Anna would want you to have him."

"Oh, yes," she said. "I know she would. Thank you. Thank you so very much."

"I can give him to you when you leave for home after the funeral, if you'd like."

"That is very kind of you," she said. "You are very kind to care for him for Anna."

"It wasn't any trouble," I said. "He's a very nice little dog."

When she started to say good-bye, I said, "Mrs. Furman? Could I ask you a few questions before you go?"

"Certainly," she said.

"Mr. Barry's son, Peter, has asked me to help investigate his death, and Anna had arranged to meet with me to talk about it. I think she knew who killed Mr. Barry, and she wanted to tell me what she knew. Did she ever talk to you about Mr. Barry's death?"

"Yes," Mrs. Furman said.

"Could you tell me what she said?"

No response.

"I know this is probably very hard for you to talk about," I said, "but it is very important. If you know anything at all, it may help to find Mr. Barry's killer, and Anna's, too. I'm almost certain the same person killed both of them. It'd be a pretty big coincidence if it was someone else.''

I heard her take a deep breath.

''And Anna wanted to help,'' I said. ''She told me that. She came to me and said she wanted to talk to me and that it was very important. If she talked to you about it, I think she would want you to tell me what you know.''

Another deep breath. ''Yes,'' she finally said. ''I will talk to you.''

Now I let out a big sigh. ''Thank you, Mrs. Furman. I know Anna would be grateful to you for any help you could give us. What did Anna say to you about Mr. Barry's death?''

''Anna admired Mr. Barry very much. She was much disturbed by his death.''

''Did she say anything about knowing who did it?''

''Yes, yes, she did.''

I let out another sigh. ''Did she tell you she knew who did it?''

''She had suspicions, yes.''

''Did she tell you what they were?''

''She told me some, yes, she did.''

Can you believe this woman?

''Mrs. Furman,'' I said, with all the patience I could muster. ''*Please.* Could you please tell me exactly what she said? What did she tell you her suspicions were? Tell me exactly what she said, as well as you can remember it.''

''Well,'' Mrs. Furman said, ''she did not tell me

the name of the person. She just tells me she suspects someone and it is someone she knows and Mr. Barry knows and she is going to do something about it. I tell her to be careful and not to do anything foolish. I tell her to go to the police…'' Mrs. Furman's voice broke and she stopped talking.

"I'm sorry, Mrs. Furman," I said gently. "You gave Anna very good advice. You did the best you could to protect her, and you're helping her now by talking to me. What you've told me is very useful. Knowing that the person she suspected was someone she and Mr. Barry both knew is very helpful."

"Do you think you can find the man who killed Anna?"

"I'm going to try as hard as I can, Mrs. Furman."

"She was the only family I had left," Mrs. Furman said.

"I know," I said. "I'm very sorry."

When she made no response, I said, "Did Anna say anything else to you about Mr. Barry's death?"

"No, no she did not. Only that she suspected someone."

"Did she talk to you about Mr. Barry before he died?"

Mrs. Furman hesitated before she answered. "No, no she did not."

"Well, I'll see you at the funeral," I said. "And we can make arrangements for you to get Scamper then."

"Thank you," she said. "Thank you very much."

I had a sudden thought. "Are you going to be taking Anna's things from her apartment while you're here?''

"Oh. Oh, my, I had forgotten about that," she said. "No, I don't think so. I will come back."

"I'd be happy to help you when you do," I said. "It's a lot for one person to do."

"Thank you," she said again. "That is very kind."

After I hung up, I made some notes in my file about our conversation and sat at my kitchen table for a while and thought about what she'd told me, and what I suspected she hadn't told me.

I didn't believe that Anna hadn't talked to Margaret about Phillip before he died, though I couldn't think why it mattered. Even if she had been in love with him and had told her sister about it, what could that possibly have to do with his death? It certainly didn't look like Anna had killed him. If she hadn't been murdered herself, it might make sense, but not now.

I went back to work on another brief and got about half an hour in when I received a phone call from Sharon Falk.

"This is Sharon Falk," she said. "I'm a CPA with Barry, Barry and Associates. Gerard Barry asked me to call you regarding the Phillip Barry matter." She hesitated for a moment. "Something about Phillip's *files?*" she added in a voice full of astonishment.

"Gerry said you were going through Phillip's files so you could give him status reports on his clients, and he wanted you to look out for anything suspicious at the same time. That's all I'm really after," I said.

"Such as?" Sharon asked, not the least bit pleasantly.

"Well, I'm not sure," I said. "I was thinking that maybe Phillip had been involved in something with a client that could have led to his death. Like he found out someone was doing something illegal and they killed him to keep him quiet."

"You realize, don't you, that our clients' affairs are confidential?"

"The only thing I'm asking you to reveal is something illegal, something someone might kill to cover up. Like embezzlement or fraud, something like that."

"You know, the police have already seen these files. Do you really believe you can find something they didn't?"

"Maybe," I said, with only the tiniest edge to my voice.

"I see," she said. "Very well then, I'll have to get back to you. I haven't gone through the files yet."

"That's fine," I said. "Thank you."

She hung up without saying good-bye. What a witch.

I still had a perturbed expression on my face when Mrs. Gunther walked in the room. She looked at me and scowled.

"Is That Homicide Detective giving you trouble again?" she asked with her hands on her hips.

I smiled and shook my head. Whenever Brian and I aren't getting along, Mrs. Gunther refers to him as "That Homicide Detective."

"No, I was just talking to one of the CPAs from Phillip's firm," I said, "and she's *extremely* uncooperative and sarcastic."

"Hmph," Mrs. Gunther said. "Maybe it's because she has something to hide."

I thought about that for a few moments. "Well, I don't know," I said.

"Unless she was doing something illegal and Phillip found out about it."

"Uh-huh," Mrs. Gunther said. She poured herself a glass of iced tea and left the room.

I decided to give Gerry a call before I went back to work.

"Is there any chance that Sharon Falk could be engaged in something illegal, such as embezzling funds from the firm?" I asked him.

He laughed so hard I nearly hung up on him. "Not a chance," he finally said, still laughing. "She's as honest as the day is long. Whatever gave you that idea?"

"Oh, nothing," I said, not entirely hiding my injured pride. "I'm just trying to be thorough."

"Well, you're certainly doing that," he said. He was still laughing, so I bade him a terse good-bye.

THE NEXT DAY was Saturday, July 19. I got up at eight-thirty, put Scamper out in the yard, brought him back in and fed him, then made myself a breakfast of sliced bananas and strawberries and a cup of tea. I took it, the dog, and my Phillip file out to my courtyard, where I have a little wrought-iron bistro table and chairs. It's not particularly comfortable, but if I really work at it, I can almost convince myself I'm in Paris at an outdoor café. I paged through my file and made notes as I went. Scamper put a paw on my knee, panted with his tongue hanging out, and lay down for a nap right next to my chair when I patted him on the head.

I made a list of all the people I'd talked to so far, and wrote down everything I thought I'd learned from them. Then I made a list of those I still wanted to see: Bob Hennison and his secretary, Sue Barry (Gerry's wife), Audrey (Phillip's and Gerry's sister), Miriam Beechman, Sandra Goldberg, and Patricia Morgan. They were all I could think of at the moment.

I finished my breakfast and decided to try reaching Patricia Morgan again. I found the number and dialed. Ten rings and no answer. Well, if I couldn't get ahold of Patricia Morgan, maybe I'd have better luck with Miriam Beechman. I decided to take a drive and see if I could find her house. Now, that was an experience.

NINE

I RAN UPSTAIRS, combed my hair, put on a little makeup, refilled Scamper's bowls, and grabbed a notebook. When I got in the car, I studied my map for a bit until I found her street. I'd been wrong. She didn't live near Mayfair. She was closer to Northridge, another big mall, way on the north side of town, the part of Milwaukee I'm not all that familiar with.

It looked like US-43 was my best bet, so I took that to Brown Deer Road and headed west to Green Bay Road. The house was a few blocks west and south of that, in a little subdivision. The roads were curved and the houses were all brown and beige. Everything looked to be about thirty years old.

I found the house easily enough, but just as I was about to pull over, a woman came from the house—she looked middle-aged, maybe forty-five or fifty, thin, long, straight blond hair, tight shorts and a T-shirt—and got into the car that was parked in the driveway. I knew it had to be her. I could either wait for her to come back or go home, I thought. *Or...I could *follow* her. No self-respecting supersleuth would pass up an opportunity like that.

I put my head down and pretended to look for something, waited until she drove by me, then turned around in her driveway and followed. *Hang back, now, don't be too obvious,* I muttered to myself as I tried to catch up to her. She kept turning corners and it was making it really hard to stay inconspicuous.

She finally made it onto a main road, drove past Hanson Park, and into Northridge Lakes. Northridge Lakes is a group of townhouses—or maybe they're condos—on a manmade lake. I followed her in, feeling more obvious by the minute, but she never seemed to take notice of me. She parked the car, got out, and went around to the back of one of the homes. I didn't want to risk getting out and following her on foot, so I parked a few doors behind her and waited. And waited. Almost fifteen minutes later, she came out again. I ducked down to get out of sight, but I could see she had a small bouquet of flowers in her hand. They looked like they'd been picked from a garden rather than purchased from a flower shop. She backed up, turned around, and drove right past me, forcing me to do the same if I wanted to keep up with her. I lost sight of her for a bit after she rounded a corner, but I caught up with her on Seventy-sixth Street. I had to weave in and out of traffic a little, because other cars kept getting between us, but I never lost her and I was never more than half a block behind. I'll tell you, if you've never followed anyone, you ought to try it. It is so cool.

We went down Seventy-sixth Street for a while, turned onto Appleton, and ended up at Holy Cross Cemetery. She drove quite a ways in, parked at the side of the road, and got out. I pulled over several hundred yards ahead of her and stayed in my car for a while and just watched. We were in what seemed like a familiar area, but I couldn't be sure. Cemetery plots all look pretty much the same to me. She walked through the grass, glancing at the tombstones, but moved purposefully as if she knew exactly where she was going. When she stopped and sat on the grass, I got out, too, and wandered over in her direction. She placed her flowers on a grave and remained seated. I couldn't hear what she was saying, but I could see her lips moving. She wasn't crying, and she didn't look particularly upset.

I was trying my best to be unobtrusive, just quietly looking at the gravestone inscriptions, when she got up and walked my way. When she glanced at me, I knelt in front of the closest grave, made a sign of the cross, and bowed my head. I didn't dare look up, but I could tell she was looking at me as she walked by.

I waited until I heard her car start, looked up very nonchalantly, and watched her drive away. When she rounded the first bend, I got up, ran over to the grave on which she'd placed the flowers, read the inscription on the stone, and bolted for my car. I caught sight of her no more than a minute later and stayed back a good distance until we left the cemetery. I followed more closely after that, but still didn't get the sense that she knew she was being followed. She drove straight home, parked in the driveway, and went right in the house.

I got out, locked my car, and rang her doorbell. When she answered the door, she gave me an odd look that quickly turned to recognition and annoyance. "Didn't I just see you in the cemetery?" she said. "What's going on here?"

I took a deep breath. "Uh, well, yes, you did," I said. "I'm sorry. I came here to talk to you and I saw you leaving so I decided to follow you."

She screwed up her face and took a step back. "What are you, some kind of a nut?" she said, and started to close her door.

"No," I said. "I'm sorry, let me explain. Really, it's all right."

"What's this all about?" she said with a sneer.

"Phillip Barry," I said.

A startled expression crossed her face and quickly disappeared. She opened her mouth to say something and closed it again and her face got really red. I love having that effect on people.

"I know you visited his grave," I said in a kind voice. "And I know you were involved with him at one time. His son Peter is very close to me and he's asked me to help him find out who murdered his father. I'm only here because I was hoping you might be able to help. You are Miriam Beechman, aren't you?" I asked, suddenly realizing I'd never made sure who she was.

She nodded, frowned, and pressed her lips together, then suddenly burst into tears. Now, I don't like having *that* effect on people.

"Would you mind if I came inside so we could talk?" I said gently.

She pushed her screen door open and let me come in. Without saying a word, she led me to the kitchen, sat down at her kitchen table, and waved at another of the chairs, which I took as an invitation to sit down.

Her kitchen was small, painted beige with a stencil

border near the ceiling. She had a round maple table with captain's chairs, and a brown refrigerator. Miriam stared out the window, which was decorated with a valance of brown gingham checks, and shook her head.

"Who told you I was involved with Phillip?" she asked without looking at me.

"Does it really matter who told me?" I said.

She let out a sigh and put a disgusted expression on her face. "No, I suppose not," she said.

"Do you mind talking to me about him?" I said. "I don't want you to feel forced."

She snorted a laugh. "Yeah, sure," she said. "Like it's going to make any difference now." She frowned and looked at me for the first time since we'd entered the house. "Why don't you just let the police take care of it? What are you getting involved for?"

I shrugged and gave her a sheepish smile. "I'm just doing it because Peter asked me to—begged me, actually. I solved another murder last winter and he's convinced I'll be able to solve this one."

Miriam arched an eyebrow. "Do tell," she said in a sarcastic voice.

I willed myself not to react. "Do you know anything about Phillip's death?" I asked.

Miriam drummed her fingers on the table and looked out the window again. "Do I know anything? No. Do I have any ideas? Maybe."

I opened my eyes wide. "What ideas do you have?"

"How much do you know about Phillip?" she asked me.

"I…know very little, really," I said, thinking that was the answer that might elicit the most information.

"Talk to anyone," she said, "and they'll all tell you the same thing. Phillip Barry was the biggest jerk this side of the Mississippi. He thought he was God's gift to women. A real first-class swine."

"Do you know anything about him that might help me figure out who killed him?" I said.

She looked at me like I was an idiot. "That's what I'm telling you," she said. "Every woman this side of Nevada wanted to kill him. I would've done it myself if I'd had the chance."

"You mean you actually think one of them did it?"

"Why not?" Miriam said. "His wife could've done it for all I know. And who'd blame her? You put me on that jury and I'd give her a prize."

"Do you know anything *else* about Phillip that might cause someone to want to kill him?"

She shook her head and looked skyward. "Look, hon, I don't know what you're looking for, but as far as I'm concerned you'll find your killer when you find the jerk's latest lover."

"Did you know Anna Schulz, by the way?"

"The secretary?" Miriam said.

I nodded.

She shook her head. "Never had the pleasure," she said.

"How long did you work for Phillip?" I asked.

"Work for him? I never *worked* for him, hon. I was married to his brother."

"You were married to Phillip's *brother*?"

One corner of Miriam's mouth turned up ever so

slightly. "I thought you knew. I was Gerry's first wife."

I couldn't believe what I was hearing. "How long ago was this?" I said.

"We got married the year before Phillip and Olivia did. That would be, what, about twenty-four years now?"

"Did Gerry know about you and Phillip?"

"Sure, he knew." She gave me a sudden smirk. "If you think Gerry killed him because of me, you're sadly mistaken. He couldn't have cared less. He never cared. Our marriage was shot long before any of that happened."

"How long were you married?"

"Four long years," Miriam said.

"How about Olivia? Did she know?"

Miriam forced a laugh. "Olivia. She never let on if she did."

"Would you do me a favor?" I said. "If you do think of anything else that might help, would you give me a call?"

"Oh, sure," she said, but she didn't sound like she meant it.

I got up, thanked her, and was just saying good-bye at the front door when I remembered something. "Why did you visit Phillip's grave," I said, "if you hated him so much?"

Miriam smirked again. "I wanted to tell him how happy I was that he was dead," she said.

I walked to my car and sat for a while. What a creepy woman. I turned on my engine and was just about to pull away from the curb when I remembered

I wanted to ask her if she knew Sandra Goldberg. I turned off the engine, ran back up to the house, and rang the bell.

"I'm sorry," I said when she answered the door. "I just remembered something else I wanted to ask you."

She glared at me and waited.

"Do you know who Sandra Goldberg is and how I might get in touch with her?"

"Never heard of her," Miriam said, and shut the door.

When I got home, I put Scamper in the yard again (he's amazingly well trained, by the way), made some Miriam notes in my Phillip file, and then read for a while. After spending more than half an hour trying to get through the same page, I decided to bag it and give Patricia Morgan another try.

Well, guess what. She was there.

TEN

"Is this the Patricia Morgan who used to work for Phillip and Gerard Barry?" I asked her.

"Yes," she said in a voice full of wariness.

I explained who I was and why I was calling, and asked if she'd be willing to talk to me about Phillip.

"Well, I suppose so," she said.

"I'd like to talk to you in person, if that's all right with you," I said.

"Uh, that's fine, I guess," she said. "I was going to do some grocery shopping but it's nothing that can't wait until later if you want to talk right away."

"Oh, that's wonderful," I said. "Are you sure? I'd be happy to wait until you finish your shopping."

She hesitated a moment. "Okay, how about this. I'll do my shopping and then I'll give you a call when I get back and you can come over to the house. It shouldn't take me any more than an hour, if that."

"That'd be great," I said. After she gave me directions, I made myself some tomato soup and took it, along with some cheddar cheese and French bread, out to my screened porch. I have a white wicker table out there with four chairs and a matching couch. I covered the cushions and some large throw pillows with coordinating fabrics, all different prints, but every one the same shade of blue and white. Along the ledges I have potted geraniums and a few pots of snow-white sweet alyssum. It's so pretty.

After I finished my lunch, I cleaned up the kitchen, brought Scamper in, and took the mystery I was reading back out to the porch while I waited for Patricia's call. "Okay, Kinsey Millhone, how would *you* find Phillip's murderer?" I said out loud. And I just sat there a while to see if I could imagine her answering back. No luck, she wasn't talking. I put down my book and went into the house to get my Phillip file when the phone rang. It was Patricia.

"Hi, I'm back," she said. "You can come anytime."

"I'll be right over," I said.

I brought a legal pad along, just in case, and headed for Hales Corners. Patricia lives just off Forest Home Avenue in the Whitnall Park area, which is a little south of West Allis, where I grew up. I've always loved Whitnall Park. We used to go there all the time when I was little. It's over five hundred acres and the Root River Parkway goes right through it. There's a golf course there, an archery range, bike trails, cross-country ski trails, the Boerner Botanical Gardens, and the Wehr Nature Center. The Boerner Gardens is forty acres all by itself, and it has every plant and flower they could possibly grow there, as well as an enormous elm tree, one of the few we have left. You can walk through and sit on little benches along the way and spend as much time as you want. The nature center has two hundred acres of preserved land and at least four miles of trails full of flowers and wildlife. There's a rose festival in the park every June; they have classes all year-round, and even concerts and art exhibits. Great cross-country skiing in the winter, too. I considered buying a house in the area once, just because of the park. Patricia Morgan was lucky enough to live right across the street from it.

"Come on in," Patricia said with a friendly smile. "We can sit out back. It's nice and cool in the yard."

"Great," I said, and followed her through the house and out her back door.

She looked to be in her mid to late thirties, with reddish-brown hair, worn short in a softly layered cut that reminded me of a hairdo that was popular when I was young. She was slender, even a bit fragile, but healthy looking at the same time. A narrow, refined nose, large blue eyes, and creamy, pale skin with lines that actually seemed to add to her good looks rather than detract from them. Like delicate etchings on fine porcelain.

The house was Lannon stone with salmon-colored trim and a light gray roof. It's sort of a Cape Cod style, but larger, with dormers on the third story. The inside, or what I saw of it, was furnished with pale oak and sage green upholstery. A very clean and light effect. The kitchen was modern, all white, probably recently redone, with light green, apricot, and light blue accents. There were a half dozen trees in her backyard, near the fence, and she had a tomato garden and a pretty elaborate flower garden near the deck.

"This is really nice," I said. "I love this area. I almost bought a house here once, but I ended up on the east side because I inherited a house from my aunt."

"Where on the east side?" Patricia asked.

"On Newberry," I said with a smile. "It's always been my favorite street, so I can't complain."

"I should say not," she said. "Well, make yourself at home and I'll get us something to drink. Would you like iced tea?"

"Sure, that'd be great," I said. I sat in one of the deck chairs covered in a salmon-striped canvas to co-ordinate with the salmon-colored awnings on the house. The trees were filled with birds engaged in some sort of bird argument. It was about eighty degrees and there was a slight breeze, so it was very pleasant in the shade.

"Here we go," Patricia said when she returned. She placed a pitcher of tea and two glasses on the table between the two chairs and poured me a glass.

"Thanks," I said. "This is a great yard."

"We've been very happy here," she said with a smile. "John—that's my husband—inherited this house from his mother when she passed away ten years ago. It took me a while to feel like it was my own, but I do now. I still felt like it was hers, in the beginning."

I laughed. "I know just what you mean," I said. "I felt the same way about my Aunt Sarah's house. She'd lived in it all my life and then suddenly it was mine, but I still felt like I was living in Aunt Sarah's house, like I didn't really belong there."

Patricia nodded and then sighed. "So you want to talk about Phillip Barry," she said. "I'd put that man out of my mind a long time ago, but I guess our sins always come back to haunt us, don't they?'' She gave me a sheepish and slightly guilty look.

I smiled.

"Well, now he's dead," she said. From the look on her face, I couldn't tell if she was glad or sad.

"You worked for the Barrys, didn't you?"

She nodded. "I was Phillip's secretary. It's only been three years since I left, but it seems like a lifetime now." She looked at me for a moment, without speaking. "I assume you know we had an affair," she said then.

I nodded.

"We worked late a lot, so we spent a lot of time together. He and his wife were having problems and John and I weren't getting along. One thing led to another and we just fell in love." Her face turned a light pink. "I know that sounds schoolgirlish now, but it seemed oh-so-serious at the time. I thought he was the love of my life and I was so sure he felt the same. I guess I should've known all along that he didn't, but I didn't want to believe it."

"Did either your husband or Phillip's wife ever find out about it?"

"Not that I'm aware of," Patricia said. "We were pretty discreet. John never noticed whether I was here or not and I think Phillip's wife was used to his late hours. It probably never occurred to either of them."

I was pretty sure it had occurred to Olivia, but I didn't say so.

"Did Phillip ever talk to you about his personal life?" I asked.

Patricia frowned. "Well, sure," she said. "If you

mean like his kids and what was going on at the office. He talked about normal things. What did you have in mind?''

"Did he ever tell you anything that might give you an idea who could've killed him?''

Patricia raised her eyebrows. "Oh,'' she said. "I see.'' She frowned and thought for a while. "I don't know,'' she said. "Not that I can think of. We did talk a lot about the business, of course. And he would discuss confidential matters with me since I'd naturally know about them anyway, but there was nothing like somebody threatening him or anything like that.''

"Did he ever tell you anything about a client that involved something illegal? Like something a client wouldn't want anyone to know about?''

"Wow, let me think. You know, we'd often do work for someone who was maybe keeping double books, or they'd skim money off the top, or fudge on their financial statements. Phillip was always a real stickler about that kind of thing. He'd talk to the client and tell them he didn't approve and they'd better clean up their act, that sort of thing. But if any of those people ever threatened him, he certainly never said anything to me about it. Besides, wouldn't this be a little late for a retaliation over something that happened so long ago?''

"Well, it probably would be,'' I said, "unless something similar occurred more recently. It's just an idea Peter put into my head. Do you remember who any of these clients were?''

"Well,'' she answered, with a somewhat reproachful look, "it really wouldn't be appropriate for me to reveal their identities. But if it'll make you feel any better, I really can't recall any of their names anyway.''

I nodded. "Okay," I said. Then I gave her a direct look. "Do you have any ideas at all about who might have killed him?"

She shook her head. "I'm sorry," she said. "I really don't. I was stunned when I read about it in the newspaper. You don't expect someone you know to get murdered. It just doesn't make sense to me. Could it have been a robbery or something like that? We had someone break into the office once and steal some of our equipment."

"No, they're sure it wasn't anything like that. There wasn't anything missing and there wasn't any sign of a break-in. And his secretary was murdered less than two weeks later, with the same gun."

"Yes, that's right," Patricia said with a frown.

"Did you know her?" I asked.

"No," Patricia said. "She must have been hired after I left."

"Oh, that reminds me. Did you know a Sandra Goldberg?"

Patricia stiffened, just a little, but answered me immediately. "Yes," she said. "Sandra Goldberg was Gerry's secretary when I was working for Phillip."

"Do you have any idea how I could get in touch with her?"

"Well, I'm not sure," Patricia said. "She quit work because she had to move back to Chicago to take care of her mother when her father died. She had Parkinson's or Alzheimer's. Something. But that was a while back. She may have died by now, and Sandra could be anywhere.''

"Are you sure it was Chicago," I said, "and not one of the suburbs?''

"No, it was definitely Chicago. She lived on the south side of Chicago. She'd go on and on about how it was so different from Milwaukee. She thought we got so much land with our houses here. Her parents' house was so close to the one next door that only one person at a time could fit through the walkway between them. They had to walk single file.''

I grinned. "That's what my Grandma Sellini's house was like. They lived in Chicago, too. You could open a window on the side of the house and practically touch the house next door.''

"It's hard to imagine," Patricia said. "But then, I have a cousin out east who thinks *we* don't have any land. It's just a matter of what you're used to, I guess.''

"Yeah. Well, I guess I'll have to look for her in Chicago and hope she hasn't moved.''

Patricia nodded and looked across the yard, as if she were thinking of something else.

"Well," I said, "I really appreciate your talking to me. If you think of anything else that might help, would you give me a call?''

"Absolutely," she said.

She walked me to the door, and we chatted a while longer before saying good-bye. When I got to my car, I wrote down, on my legal pad, everything she had told me, and added a few impressions of my own. I drove about three blocks toward home, and decided to turn around. I hadn't been to Whitnall Park yet that summer and I was in the mood for a walk through the gardens. I took my pad with me when I got there, found a quiet bench, and made some additional notes about my investigation and what I planned to do next. Then I just sat for a while and enjoyed the sun and the perfume of the flowers. I could hear insects buzzing about, a light breeze through the trees, a bird tweeting to himself, and soft voices in the distance. I leaned my head against the back of the bench and closed my eyes and just listened to the sounds. The Botanical Gardens is such a peaceful place.

A few minutes later, the soft voices got louder and I was no longer alone. A man, probably in his fifties, wearing plaid Bermuda shorts and an Izod shirt, walked by with two young boys (also wearing plaid shorts and white knit shirts). He nodded and smiled, said hello, and followed behind his boys at a leisurely pace.

I took a stroll then myself, looked at all my favorite flowers, and decided to go home. I wanted to see if I could get ahold of Sandra Goldberg.

It was three-thirty when I got there. I let the dog out, *again,* made myself a pitcher of iced tea, and had one glass with some strawberries and blueberries before I called Chicago information.

I wasn't seriously expecting to get a number at all. Instead, I got three. A man answered at the first number, told me his wife had never worked in Milwaukee, and certainly not for an *accountant.* When I dialed the second number, I got an answering machine. I decided not to leave a message yet, until I tried the third number. I dialed it and got no answer so I re-dialed the second number and left a message, asking the Sandra Goldberg of the house to call me collect if she were the one I was looking for.

Well, that was all I could do for the time being. No use sitting around on a beautiful summer day waiting for the phone to ring. I called Mrs. Robinson to remind her of our dinner date the next day. She'd requested a roast beef dinner I make with carrots, po-tatoes, onions, and gravy—and biscuits, of course. And a fresh peach pie. I called Janice next, and asked her if she'd like to go bike riding with me near the lake.

"Sure," she said. "I'd love to."

"Great. I'll be in the backyard in my garden. Just come and get me."

I put on some comfortable shorts, a T-shirt, and my sneakers, and went out in the yard. Scamper was tak-ing a nap in the sun so I decided to put his bowls outside so I could leave him there while I was out with Janice. I went back inside and got them, and then went over and scowled at my flowers. I just started trying to grow some of my own this year. My Aunt Sarah already had quite a few perennials—three big lilac bushes, pink and white peonies, tiger lilies, a beautiful purple clematis on a trellis, seven kinds of roses, and those lavender flowers that pop when you squeeze them. I have a yard service that takes care of my lawn, and I pay them a little extra to take care of the flowers, too. They seemed to like Aunt Sarah's just fine but when I showed them mine they just smiled politely and said they'd do their best. They also said something about having to plant things at the right time of year, and in the right spot, and not too close together.

"Oh, your flowers look so pretty," Janice said when she walked into my yard.

I gave her a tentative smile. "Thanks," I said. "It's nice to have someone appreciate them."

"How could anyone not appreciate them?"

"Well, what I don't understand is why they get so tall and then they just flop over like this. I can't even get them to stand up. Look at these things. They sure didn't look like this in the picture they had on the package."

Janice wrinkled her nose. "Maybe you should tie them to a stick."

"You think so?"

She shrugged. "I don't know, it might work."

"Well, I guess I could try that," I said. "But not now. Let's got for a ride."

I got my bike out of the garage and helped Janice remove hers from the rack.

"You want to just ride down to the lake and get on the walkway? The beach stands'll be open if we get thirsty or something."

"Sure." Janice said.

We went a couple of blocks down Newberry to Lake Park, then straight through to Lincoln Memorial Drive. We got off the street right away and onto the sidewalk (Lake Drive's a pretty busy road and I don't feel safe riding in the street), rode past Bradford Beach, past McKinley Beach, and then all the way down to the War Memorial, where we jumped off our bikes to rest for a while. The air was nice and cool, as it always is right on the lake (it's probably ten degrees cooler there than in Wauwatosa, where my parents live).

We could see the Summerfest grounds—officially known as the Henry Maier Festival Park—from where we stood. Milwaukee has almost a dozen festivals in that park every summer (hence our nickname, "The City of Festivals"), and we get quite an influx from neighboring states for everyone of them. There's the Asian Moon Festival in the spring, Polish Fest in June, Summerfest for eleven days in late June to early July, Festa Italiana the third weekend of July, German Fest the last weekend in July, African World Festival at the beginning of August, Irish Fest the third weekend in August, Mexican Fiesta the fourth weekend in August, and Indian Summer the second weekend in September. My favorite is Irish Fest. It's the largest Irish festival in the world, and many of the performers come all the way from Ireland.

You can never be at a loss for something to do in the summer here. There's always something going on. In addition to the festivals, there's the State Fair in August (another big attraction to Illinois as well as Wisconsin residents), Rainbow Summer at the Performing Art Center's outdoor Peck Pavilion from June through August, Bastille Days for four days in July, and the Great Circus Parade in mid-July. The circus parade is absolutely the best parade in the entire world. Ernest Borgnine agrees. He comes every year.

"Did you go to Summerfest this year?" I asked Janice.

"No," she said. "I always went with Dave. It just wouldn't have been the same, you know?"

I gave her a sympathetic smile. "I'll go with you next year. He'd want you to go."

Janice looked off into the distance for a few moments. When she looked back at me, her lip quivered and she had tears in her eyes. "Okay," she said. "I will go with you. You're right, he would want me to go."

"You want to get something to drink?" I asked.

"Sure," she said. "Let's get some ice cream, too."

We walked our bikes to the nearest beach stand, bought Cokes and double chocolate ice cream cones (a strange combination, I found out), and found a place to sit and relax. The sky was a deep blue, with little wisps of clouds, and the lake was calm and sparkly.

"I just love it here," I said. "You know, I think it's so weird when people say nature makes them feel small and insignificant. It always makes me feel just the opposite."

Janice smiled and watched a sea gull fly high in the sky. "Yeah, me, too," she said.

When we got back to my house, I had a message on my machine. I let Scamper in first, because he was barking, and then I played it back. It was from Sandra Goldberg.

ELEVEN

"OH, MY GOSH, I found her," I said to Janice.

"Who?" she said.

"Sandra Goldberg. She's one of the women Phillip Barry had an affair with. She lives in Chicago and I wasn't sure if I had the right one. Do you mind if I call her back?"

"No," she said. "Go ahead. You have any iced tea?"

"In the refrigerator."

Janice went to the kitchen and I dialed Sandra Goldberg's number.

She wasn't home.

"Well, she's not there," I said. "You want something to eat?"

"What do you have?"

I opened the refrigerator. "Cheese—cheddar and pepper jack—blueberries, strawberries, watermelon, peaches, and yogurt." I closed the refrigerator and opened my jelly cupboard. "Triscuits, Sociables, and just regular crackers. And then I have these mustard-flavored pretzels."

"Ooh, I love those. How about pretzels, Triscuits and Sociables, and cheese."

I laughed. "Which kind?"

"Both?" Janice said.

"Sounds good to me."

We had a little feast and talked until six, when Janice decided to head home. I helped her get her bike back on her car and told her I'd see her on Monday.

It was time I got ready for Anna Schulz's wake.

I filled Scamper's bowls again, took a quick shower, and opened my closet. Same old problem. What to wear? You know, what I really need is a regular wake/funeral wardrobe, just a few subdued black and blue things, a couple for every season. After rejecting everything else in my closet, I put on the same dress I'd worn to Phillip's wake and figured no one would notice. I fixed myself a cup of tea to drink in the car, gave the dog a little kiss on his warm little head, and took off.

Peter and Olivia were at the funeral home when I arrived (but neither Paul nor Haley), along with Gerry, Joanne Donnelly, Sharon Falk, Anna's sister, and, of course, Brian. There was one wreath of flowers near the casket, with a banner: *Beloved Sister*. Margaret Furman didn't look anything like I'd expected her to. She was about fifty years old, not younger than I, as I'd thought, and she had brassy dyed-blond hair worn at the nape of her neck in a braided bun. Her dress was black crepe, with shiny spots from too much ironing, and she had a black lace veil on her head. I introduced myself and she thanked me for trying to help Anna and for taking care of Scamper. I invited her to come to my house the next day after the funeral to pick him up, and she accepted.

Brian nodded politely to me when I came in, and looked in another direction as if we were mere acquaintances. He spent the entire evening in the back of the room, scanning the faces, watching every little movement. He was pretty obvious, but I suppose it didn't matter. No one was giving anything away, from what I could see. I'd intended to at least say goodbye to him, but when I turned around to find him near the end of the service, he was already gone.

"Well, I met Anna's sister tonight," I said to Scamper when I got home. His ears perked up and he padded over to me and put a paw on my knee. I scratched him behind the ears and patted his head, and he jumped into my lap. He stayed there for a long time and fell fast asleep, while I stared out the window into the night.

THE NEXT DAY was Sunday, July 20, the day of Anna's funeral—and the day I had to give up Scamper. I got up extra early, had breakfast with my soon-to-be-absent dog, and drove to the church. Everyone from the office showed up—Gerry, Joanne Donnelly, the receptionist, Sharon Falk, and two other women I'd never seen before—but that was it except for me, Anna's sister, and That Homicide Detective.

At the cemetery, Brian came up from behind me and squeezed my shoulder. I turned and gave him an uncertain smile and he gave me an even more uncertain one back. You know, I really hate this dating thing. It's even worse than marriage.

The priest said a few words about Anna and her life, and Anna's sister cried silent tears the whole way through. When the burial service was over, Brian whispered "I'll call you later" in my ear, and took off after Gerry and Sharon Falk. I went to Margaret and told her I'd see her whenever she could make it.

"Thank you," she said, after she blew her nose into a dainty embroidered handkerchief. "I will be there soon."

I smiled, gently patted her on the arm, and went home.

What a horrible day. I hate funerals so much and I'd been to two in the last two weeks. "Come here, Scamper," I said when I walked into the kitchen. He'd been lying in his bed and he perked up his ears when I called his name. As soon as he looked into my eyes, I started to cry. He tilted his head and gave me a curious look, as if he wasn't sure what to make of this new behavior, and then he padded over and put his head in my lap. I picked him up and hugged him and cried into his fur, and he didn't even squirm.

"I'm going to miss you, you little fuzzy guy," I said.

He lifted his head and licked my face with his sandpaper tongue. "Yuck, dog germs," I said, and he did it again.

An hour later, Margaret showed up. I brought her into the kitchen where Scamper was sleeping again, and offered her a seat. "Would you like a cup of tea?" I said.

"That would be very nice," she answered. She was watching Scamper, who hadn't waked up, and she looked about ready to cry.

"Have you seen him before?"

"Oh, yes," she said. "Many times when I come to visit Anna. Anna had Scamper many years."

I smiled, gave Margaret her tea, and sat down with mine in the chair next to hers. I didn't really know what to say. I just sighed and Margaret looked at me.

"What have you learned about Anna's murder?" she said.

"Well," I said, feeling unaccountably guilty, "I'm not sure. I still don't know who did it but I've come up with some ideas, at least. It's too early to do anything, though. I need to learn a lot more before I could feel comfortable accusing anyone."

She nodded. "I see," she said with a sigh, and stared into her cup.

"I won't give up until I know who did it," I said, "and neither will the police. Don't worry, we'll find him."

Margaret gave the teacup a brief smile, but said nothing.

"Would you like another cup of tea?" I said, "or something to eat?"

"No, thank you," she said.

Scamper was doing that doggy-dream thing that he does all the time (which is really weird) and I willed him to wake up. When willing didn't work, I made an extra lot of noise with my chair when I got up to rinse out our cups, and that did the trick.

"Hey, Scamper," I said. "Look who's here."

He looked at me, then at Margaret, and back at me. "It's Margaret," I said. "Anna's sister." At the mention of Anna, his ears went up and his eyes got brighter.

"Here, Scamper," Margaret said, and he walked right over and licked her hand. "Would you like to come to the big State of Texas and live with me?"

He said, "No, I want to stay right here and live with Beth," but I don't think she heard him.

"That's a good boy," she said.

"How are you going to get him home?" I asked her.

"I have spoken to the airline and they will take care of it," she said. "He will be fine in the cab to the airport."

"Do you want to take his bed? He'd really miss it if you didn't."

"Of course," she said, and scratched his head. "Anna made that for him herself. Well, I must go now. My flight is in an hour."

"Would you like a ride to the airport?" I said. "It's no trouble at all."

She hesitated a moment, and said, "That is very kind of you."

We put Scamper's things, including the dog food I had left, in a large shopping bag she could carry on, and I carried Scamper to the car. I hugged him so tightly, he barked at me.

When we got to the airport, I gave him a teary kiss and told him I loved him and I'd miss him.

Margaret thanked me, gave me a kind smile, and left.

Brian called about an hour after I got home. "What's the matter?" he said when he heard my voice.

"Scamper's gone," I said. "Margaret Furman took him home with her to Texas."

He didn't respond for a moment. "You got kind of attached to him, huh?" he said then.

"Yeah," I answered.

"Want me to come over?"

I hesitated. "Okay," I said, sounding more uncertain than I felt.

"Are you sure?" Brian said. "You don't sound particularly thrilled with the idea."

"I'm sorry," I said. "I really do want you to come over. I'm just depressed, that's all. And you can't stay very long anyway, because I have to get everything ready for Mrs. Robinson's dinner."

"Well, maybe I can help you with that. I'll be right there."

"Great," I said with a smile. I was feeling a little better already.

Brian was there in half an hour. He cut up the potatoes and the onions, while I did the carrots and the peaches, and he insisted on helping me make the pie. He got flour all over the kitchen and himself and me, but it was fun anyway. If I started to look sad, he distracted me. He was acting like his old self again, and that made me very happy. When it was time for me to go, he kissed me good-bye (first time in quite a while), and said he'd call the next day. When he left, I missed *him* almost as much as I missed Scamper.

I ran upstairs, changed into culottes and a T-shirt, had a cup of tea, and headed for Brady Street.

Mrs. Robinson had her door wide open, as usual,

so I knocked on the doorjamb and walked right in. I could hear her in the kitchen but I was pretty sure she hadn't heard me. I walked back to find her and tried to make some noise as I went so I wouldn't startle her when she saw me.

"Is that you, Beth?" she said from around the corner.

"It's me," I answered back. I came in, put my things on the kitchen table, and gave her a big hug and a kiss. "How are you?" I said.

"I'm just wonderful," she said. "I always am on the days you're here." She grabbed hold of my arms and looked at me with a fond smile, and then gave me another hug.

"I'm going to get this started right away," I said. "It takes about an hour to cook."

"And I'm going to sit down," she said. "I've been on my feet just a mite too long."

"Would you like me to make you a cup of tea?" I asked.

"That would be lovely, my dear. Just lovely."

"Okay, I'll be right in."

I put the vegetables and beef in the oven and set the timer for forty minutes so I'd have enough time to make the biscuits and have them bake along with everything else. I heated two cups of water in the microwave, added tea bags, and brought them out to the living room on a tray. I placed one on the table next to Mrs. Robinson's chair, and sat down on the couch with mine.

She dipped her tea bag in and out several times, wrapped it around the spoon to squeeze out every last drop, and put it on the tray. She took a sip, and then another, and sighed. "This is just what I needed," she said. "Thank you, my dear."

"You're welcome," I said with a smile. She looked extra tired, and it worried me a little. Sometimes I start to think about what it would be like if she died—which, of course, I know she will someday—and I can hardly stand it. I know it sounds terrible, and I think my mother's actually suspected it, but in some ways I feel closer to Mrs. Robinson than I do to my own mother. I think it's partly because she's so vulnerable and she seems to need me so much. A pretty selfish reason, I suppose, but it does make a difference.

"Tell me about your week," she said when she'd had a little more tea. "I want to know all about your investigation. Have you had any leads?" She giggled with expectation.

I laughed. "Well, it's hard to say," I said. "He seems to have been very popular with the women, even his own brother's wife."

Mrs. Robinson frowned and made a *tsk*ing sound.

"Did I tell you his secretary was murdered, too? Her funeral was this morning."

"Oh, my. Yes, I believe you did," she said. "Do you think it was the same killer?"

"I'm assuming it was," I said. "It'd be an awfully big coincidence if it wasn't."

"Yes, it would," Mrs. Robinson said. "Unless," she added, "the second killer had always planned to kill the secretary and saw this as his chance to make it look like someone else did it."

"Well, I guess that's possible," I said. "Although it looks like they were both killed with the same gun, and she really wanted to talk to me about her boss's murder. She even told her sister that she thought she knew who did it."

"Oh, I see. Yes, I think you're right, in that case. It's definitely the same killer. Definitely." Mrs. Robinson frowned and looked like she was thinking hard, so I waited.

"What else have you found out?" she said, with a very serious look.

"Well, his wife apparently knew about his affairs but let him get away with it. She and his kids inherit a lot of money, but Olivia—that's his wife—really has a lot of her own so I don't think that's much of a motive. And the kids don't even get theirs until they turn twenty-one."

"How old are the children?" she asked.

"Peter's sixteen, Haley's nineteen, and Paul is twenty."

She frowned. "When will Paul be twenty-one?"

I raised my eyebrows. "I don't know," I said. "You mean you think he could have done it just to get his inheritance?" What an appalling thought.

"I have heard of worse things in my time," Mrs. Robinson said. "When I was a girl, there was a family who lived in our neighborhood, a very respectable family. Or so we thought," she added with a telling look. "One day...now I have to think. This was in nineteen-eighteen, I believe, and it was in the autumn, as I recall, because the leaves were just turning, and the father and the mother were both found locked in the shed in the back of the house. And, of course, they were dead, poisoned to death. Came a week later, the police determined that the boy had done it. He said it was because they sent him to bed without any supper.'' Mrs. Robinson shook her head. ''I still don't know how he got them into that shed.''

I shuddered. ''Wow,'' I said. ''What a horrible story.''

''Yes,'' she said. ''It *is* a horrible story. But that is why I think you should find out when that young man's birthday is.'' She nodded her head as if she'd settled everything.

We chatted for about ten more minutes about this and that and then the timer went off. (Or, as my niece, Katy, once said to me when she was three years old, it went *on* first and then I *turned* it off.) I made the biscuits and put them in the oven, reset the timer, and came back out. We talked some more about the case (she also suggested I keep an eye on Gerry for any suspicious behavior) and then had our dinner.

''I've never had such delicious food,'' Mrs. Robinson said. She always says that, but I love hearing it every time. ''And I've never had such wonderful company.''

I reached over and gave her a hug. ''Neither have I,'' I said.

I stayed until around seven, as I always do, so we could chat some more. Mrs. Robinson asked me to keep her posted on my investigation, and I said I would.

When I got home, I checked my messages. There was only one, and it was from Nicole Friedman, wanting to know if I'd made any progress on the case. I called her back and told her I hadn't, and made a note regarding her call in my file. It puzzled me. I couldn't understand why she seemed so concerned.

TWELVE

THE NEXT DAY, Monday, July 21, I called Gerry, first thing.

"Gerry, why didn't you tell me you used to be married to Miriam Beechman?" I said.

I heard him sigh. "I don't know," he said. "I don't know why I didn't tell you."

Great. Just the answer I was looking for.

"How did you find out about her affair with Phillip?" I said.

"I thought you talked to her. Why didn't you ask her?"

"I'm interested in hearing your side of the story."

Dead silence.

"Hello?" I said.

"Yeah, sure," he said. "It's just...there's nothing to tell. It was a long time ago. I married her right after college and it only lasted four years. It was a big mistake from the start. We both knew it, and Phillip knew I didn't care. It wasn't like he was taking something I wanted."

"But I still don't understand why you didn't tell me who she was."

"I don't know why," he said with an exasperated tone. "Maybe I was embarrassed, I don't know. I gave you her name. Isn't that enough?"

I sighed. "Yeah, I guess."

"Did you learn anything from her?" he said.

"She thinks Olivia did it. Or if she didn't, she thinks she should have."

Gerry laughed a little uncomfortably. "Olivia took an awful lot of grief from Phillip. I often wondered why she put up with it."

I spent a few more unproductive minutes talking to him and hung up when I heard Mrs. Gunther come in.

"It's going to be a hot one," she said, and wiped her face with the bandanna she usually wears to keep her hair back. "*Ninety-two,* they said on the radio. We'll have tornado warnings tonight, you mark my words."

"Wonderful," I said. "I can hardly wait."

"I'm going to crank the cooler up, if you don't mind," she said. "I can't work in this heat."

"Sure, go ahead," I said. "Put it wherever it's comfortable for you."

Janice and Emily came in a few minutes later. I joined them in the library after I put in a call to Sandra Goldberg (not home) and made myself a second cup of tea. We worked until one, had a lunch with Mrs. Gunther of cold chicken legs, tomato and onion salad, and French bread, and worked some more until five-thirty. We had nothing really pressing that week, which was nice given the crunch of the two weeks before, so they took off for home and I actually quit for the day. I was hungry again, so I made a supper of chicken salad from the leftover chicken, with mayonnaise and a little pickle relish on rye bread (my favorite sandwich when I was a kid).

Brian called at six and asked how I was feeling. His voice was sweet and caring and kind. Just like the old Brian.

"I'm okay," I said. "Thanks for coming over yesterday. You really made me feel a lot better."

"Good," he said. "How was the dinner with Mrs. Robinson?"

"Great. She says you should find out when Paul turns twenty-one. She thinks he might've killed Phillip to get his inheritance."

Brian didn't answer for a moment. "He'll be twenty-one in November," he said, but now his voice was tinged with tension and barely controlled anger.

"Does Mrs. Robinson have any other theories?" he asked. Now he was sounding sarcastic.

"No," I said quietly. "She did think you ought to keep an eye on Gerry, though."

"Well, thank her for me, will you? I'll talk to you later." And he hung up. Darn!

I tried to read, though I had a very hard time of it. I was busy feeling quite sorry for myself when Sandra Goldberg called at seven-fifteen. Her voice was tentative and barely audible.

"I'm expecting my husband any minute," she said. "I'm sorry I didn't call sooner, but I don't want him to know I'm talking to you."

"That's okay," I said. "I understand. Does your husband know anything about Phillip?"

"He doesn't even know who he is," she said. "We weren't married when I knew Phillip, but I don't know how he'd react if he knew I'd been involved with a married man. That isn't going to come out if I talk to you, is it?''

I hesitated a moment. ''Well, I'm certainly not going to say anything about it,'' I said. ''But if you know something that could help solve the murder, you really should tell the police.''

''I'm sure I don't know anything like that,'' she said.

''Would you mind talking to me about Phillip? I'm not with the police, so you're certainly not obligated to, but Phillip's son, Peter, asked me to help find the murderer, so I'd really appreciate it if you would.''

''I don't mind,'' she said in a kind voice. ''I didn't even know about the murder until you called, but I've been thinking about it ever since.''

''Oh, my gosh, I'm so sorry,'' I said. ''I forgot that you might not know since you live in Chicago.''

''It's okay,'' she said. ''It's not as if we were close. Not now, anyway.''

''I understand you had to leave the firm to take care of your mother.''

''Yes, I had to come home after my father died. My mother's ninety-one and she has Alzheimer's, so she really can't be left alone.''

''Can you tell me what went on between you and Phillip? Did it end because you had to leave?''

''No,'' she said. ''It ended because I saw him with another woman.''

Patricia Morgan was my bet. ''Was it Phillip's secretary?'' I asked.

''Phillip's secretary?'' she said. ''You mean he was involved with her, too?''

"Well, I don't know," I said. "I was just guessing."

"Oh. Well, no, it was another accountant."

I wrinkled my brow and thought for a moment. "You mean an accountant from another firm?"

"No," Sandra said. "She was with the firm. Her name was Sharon Falk."

"Are you sure about that?" I said. "Couldn't they have been working and you misunderstood?"

"Believe me," Sandra said. "What I saw could not have been taken any other way."

I wasted a few moments while I let that one sink in. "Did you ever observe or hear anything that would give you an idea who might have killed Phillip?" I asked. "Like problems he might've had with anyone? Enemies he might've made?"

"No," she said. "I'm sorry."

"That's okay," I said. "You've been very helpful. Unless you can think of anything else that might help, I'll let you go before your husband comes home."

"Thanks," she said. "I can't, offhand, but if I do I promise I'll call again."

"Thank you," I said. "Thank you very much."

Well, that was a revelation or two. I got out my Phillip file, wrote down everything Sandra had told me, added my own thoughts and interpretations, and then read through my whole file once again. I really needed to talk with Sharon Falk. And Gerry. My bet was he knew all about Sharon and Phillip and resolutely neglected to put her on his little list.

I WOKE UP very tired the next morning, took an extra long shower, drank an extra cup of tea, and called

Gerry at nine-fifteen.

"Did you know that Sharon Falk was having an affair with Phillip at the same time Sandra Goldberg was? Patricia Morgan, too, now that I think of it. He certainly kept himself busy, didn't he?"

No response.

"Gerry?"

Still no response, and then a deep sigh. "Where did you learn that?" he said in a really steely voice.

I wasn't sure I should tell him, but I couldn't think why it should matter. "Sandra Goldberg told me," I said.

Silence again, except for another big breath. "I'll get back to you," Gerry said, and hung up.

I called right back and asked for Sharon Falk.

"Ms. Falk's office," a voice said.

When I asked to speak to Ms. Falk, the voice, which I learned belonged to Eunice Waters, Sharon Falk's secretary, told me that Ms. Falk would be out of the office until the end of the week.

I explained to Eunice Waters who I was and what I was doing. "Would *you* be willing to talk to me about this?" I asked her.

She groaned, then paused for several moments before answering. "I'm really terribly busy," she said with a whine. "I hope it won't take too much time."

"It won't, I promise. Could I come over and talk to you now?"

Another, even lengthier pause. "I suppose so," she said.

EUNICE WAS SEATED at her desk when I got there, reading a magazine. She's about fifty, I would guess, with dyed hair that I'm sure is meant to be blond, but it's really closer to a light orange. The texture's a little like straw. She wears makeup that leaves a telltale line under her chin, and bright green eye shadow. Her eyebrows are dark and her eyes are deep-set and brown. She has very narrow, thin legs, and is heavy everywhere else, kind of like a bird.

"Eunice?" I said.

She looked up and arched her eyebrows.

"Hi, I'm Beth Hartley. Is there somewhere we could talk privately?"

Big sigh. "I suppose we can use Ms. Falk's office," she said in a voice infused with martyrdom. She raised herself up, pushing off from the desk, and massaged her lower back as she walked. I followed her into the office and closed the door behind me. She cleared a space on the end of the couch and sat down.

"I promise I'll make this fast," I said, as I leaned against the arm of one of the chairs. She put on a weary face and waited.

"Did Anna ever say anything to you about Phillip's death?"

Eunice shrugged and put her whole body into it. "Sure," she said. "She was upset, naturally. He was her boss."

"Did she say anything to indicate she might know who killed him?"

"Like what, for instance?"

"Anything," I said. "Did she say anything at all about suspecting someone?"

Eunice shook her head. "She never said a word. Just be careful, that's all she said."

I frowned. "She told you to be careful? Do you know what she meant by that?"

"How should I know?" Eunice said. "She told everyone to be careful."

"Has Ms. Falk ever indicated that *she* suspects anyone?"

Eunice wrinkled her brow and gave me a puzzled look. "No, she never said a word."

"Have you ever observed anything strange around here, anything that you think might be relevant to either murder?"

"Not a thing," she said, and gave me a blank stare. I sighed and forced a smile. "Well, thanks, Eunice," I said. "If you do happen to think of something, would you let me know?"

"Sure, sure," she said.

I said good-bye and let myself out.

I was about to head for home when something occurred to me. Gerry's door was open but his head was down so I knocked lightly on the doorjamb and he looked up.

"Beth," he said with a look of surprise. "Come in."

"I won't be a minute," I said. "I was just here talking to Eunice but I remembered I wanted to ask you about Bob Hennison. Have you found out yet when he'll be back?"

"Yes, as a matter of fact, I talked to him last night. He'll be back in the office on Monday morning."

Almost a full week away. "And his secretary's on vacation until he comes back?"

"That's right," Gerry said.

I gave him a plaintive look. "Would you mind if I called her at home?" I said. "I'd really like to talk to her before Monday, if you don't mind."

He put a pensive look on his face and regarded me for a moment. "All right," he said. "I'll give you her number." He flipped through a Rolodex, scribbled something on the back of a card, and handed it to me.

"Thanks," I said with an appreciative smile. "I'll talk to you later."

WHEN I GOT HOME, I poked my head in the library to say "Hi" to Janice and Em, made myself a cup of tea, and dialed Louise Beaumont's (Bob Hennison's secretary's) number. I introduced myself when she answered the phone, went through my usual explanation, and asked if I might speak to her in person.

"Well, I don't see how I can help you," she said, "but I'm certainly willing to try. I was just about to have a bite of lunch but you could come here to the house at one-twenty, if that would suit you."

"That would be just fine," I said. "Thank you very much."

It was just a little after noon, so I made myself a somewhat early lunch after receiving a "no" from both Janice and Emily to my invitation to join me. I brought my Phillip file into the kitchen and read through it as I ate, making notes on a separate pad as I thought of questions to ask Louise.

At twelve-forty-five, I told Em and Janice good-bye and headed for Vliet Street. Louise Beaumont lived in an old, rather modest neighborhood, with tiny houses and very few trees. Her house was white, with aluminum siding, a small stoop, but no front porch. I parked on the street, two doors down, walked up, and rang the doorbell. She took quite a few minutes to answer but I recognized her as soon as I saw her. She was one of the women I'd seen at Anna's funeral. She was about sixty years old, quite thin, with a beauty-parlor hairdo that reminded me a little of cotton candy. She was wearing light blue knit slacks, a white knit shirt, and pink sneakers.

"Yes?" she said in a cautious voice as she opened the door just a crack.

When I told her who I was, she opened the door a bit wider, but barely enough for me to fit through. Her living room, which was quite small, looked like something out of the 1950s. Every bit of furniture was blond wood with those narrow, tapered legs. There was a lava lamp on one of the end tables and a sunburst clock on the sofa wall. As hard as I tried, I couldn't keep from grinning, but she didn't seem to notice.

She offered me a seat on the couch (she called it the divan) and she took a chair across from and facing me. She folded her hands in her lap and looked at me as if I were in the third grade and she were my teacher. "Now then, what can I do for you?" she said.

"Well," I said, "as you know, I'm trying to determine who killed both Phillip Barry and Anna

Schulz, so my first question is, do you have any idea who might have done it?''

"None," she said, and patiently waited for my next question.

"Did you know either of them very well?"

"I never socialize in the office," she said primly. "I feel it's inappropriate."

"Oh," I said. (I couldn't really think of a better response.) "How long have you worked for Mr. Hennison?"

"For seven and one half years," Louise said. "I came with him when he joined Barry, Barry and Associates." She lowered her eyelids a bit and raised her chin.

"Well, that's very nice," I said, trying to ward off a smirk. "Mr. Hennison must value you very highly."

She just smiled and adopted a smug expression.

"Is he doing important work out of the country?" I asked.

"Oh, yes," she said. "He's presenting several very important papers in Scotland. He's quite well respected, you know."

"I'm sure he is," I said. "How long has he been with the firm, did you say?"

"Two years," Louise said.

"So I don't suppose he knew Mr. Barry very well. Or Anna Schulz, either."

She lowered her eyelids again and gave them a little flutter. "Well, I'm *certain* he didn't know Miss Schulz on a personal level but, of course, he and Mr. Barry were quite close. Mr. Barry had the greatest respect for Mr. Hennison, and he for him. He was quite stunned to hear of his death.''

''I'm sure he was,'' I said. ''Had he been in Scotland long when Mr. Barry died?''

''He'd only left the night before,'' she said sadly. ''It was quite a shame because, of course, he couldn't come back. His first paper was scheduled to be delivered the day after the body was discovered and the next one only two days later. It was quite out of the question for him to return at that time.''

I nodded. ''Well,'' I said, ''I hope I'll have a chance to talk to him when he gets back. Do you think he'll have time to fit me in?''

''Mr. Hennison is a very busy man,'' she said with lowered lids. ''But I'll discuss the matter with him and see if something can be arranged.''

''I'd appreciate that,'' I said. Then I got up to leave.

She stood, too, and walked briskly toward the door, opened it quite wide this time, and said, ''Good-bye.''

''Good-bye,'' I said with an amused smile.

THE NEXT DAY was Wednesday, July 23. Mrs. Gunther came in at eight because she needed to leave early to take her sister Erma to the doctor, and Janice and Emily both showed up at nine. After everyone was settled, I called Gerry again. I wanted to talk to his wife (assuming *she* was willing), but I wanted to find out, first, if Gerry had any objections.

''No,'' he said. ''Of course not. But I'm not sure it's going to be worth your while. I don't know what she can tell you that I haven't.''

Maybe so, I thought, but it was always interesting to have another person's perspective. "Well, it can't hurt to try," I said.

"Uh-huh," Gerry said, and gave me his home phone number. "You won't get her until after four. She's a nurse at St. Luke's and she's on duty till three."

I had an uneventful day of work, lunch, work. At four-fifteen, I called Sue Barry.

"Would you mind talking to me about Phillip?" I asked, after I'd explained the reason for my call. "Peter especially told me to talk to you and his Aunt Audrey. I get the impression he feels pretty close to you both."

"Yes," Sue said in a voice full of warmth. "We've always been the best of friends. He's a real charmer, that one."

"He sure is," I said with a laugh.

"I'd be glad to do anything I can," she said. "Would you like to come to the house? Gerry won't be home for hours and the kids are at camp so we'd have plenty of privacy."

"Sure, that'd be great," I said.

After she gave me directions, I ran upstairs and changed, had a quick cup of tea, and headed for Brookfield, another somewhat well-to-do area of Waukesha County, a little to the west of Wauwatosa.

Sue and Gerry live in one of the older sections of the city, in a fieldstone ranch set back a good distance from the road. A lot more modest than Phillip's and Olivia's place.

Sue is about five-five with short, permed blond hair

and glasses. A little on the plump side, but kind of cute, I thought. I guessed her to be about forty-five years old. She was wearing red Bermuda shorts and a red and white striped T-shirt. She smiled in a very friendly way when she opened the door and I liked her immediately.

"Come in," she said. "I hope you'll excuse the mess. I've been sewing and I haven't had a chance to clean up."

"Oh, that's all right," I said. "What are you making?"

"Come and see," she said, clearly delighted that I'd asked. Her sewing machine was set up in her dining room and her fabric and sewing supplies were laid out on the dining room table. The living room and dining room were small, but friendly and cozy. The couch was light blue and the two big easy chairs a blue and wine-colored stripe. There were two oak end tables and a matching coffee table, and an oak dining room set. The floors were hardwood, the drapes a dark red and blue plaid. A rocking chair sat on a blue braided rug, facing the fireplace, which was made of fieldstone like the exterior of the house.

"It's for Tara, my seven-year-old," Sue said. "She's going to a birthday party on Saturday and she wanted a special dress. I'm almost finished with it. All it needs are the buttons and the hem." She held the dress up for me to see, with a proud smile. "What do you think?" she said, her face beaming. "Oh, my gosh, it's absolutely beautiful," I said, with complete sincerity. "It must've taken you weeks to do this."

She smiled as hugely as humanly possible and managed a shy thank you.

"It must be so nice to have a little girl to sew for," I said.

"It really is," Sue said. "I just hope she likes it. She's getting older and they start developing their own tastes, you know. I dread the day they'll both come home with safety pins through their noses and tattoos all over their bodies."

I laughed. "You have a girl and a boy? I think that's what Peter said."

"Yes, Joel is fourteen. He has one of those new haircuts," she said with a wrinkled nose. "With a tail. I don't know why I give in but I always do."

"Well, it's a lot better than safety pins, look at it that way," I said with a wry smile.

"Well, now that's true," she said. "Come on, let's go into the kitchen. It's a lot less cluttered in there."

I followed her into a kitchen about the same size as my mother's. The walls and cabinets were painted white, and the knobs were navy blue. Her oval table and chairs were white, too, with ruffles around the seats and matching cushions in a navy and white flowered print. The café curtains were made of the same fabric.

"What a cute kitchen," I said. "You didn't do all this, too, did you?"

"Guilty as charged," she said with a timid smile. "I wasn't sure how it was going to look, but it turned out better than I expected. I'm pretty happy with it."

"Well, you're very talented," I said. "Gerry's a lucky guy."

She hesitated, just a bit, before she smiled. And there was a sadness to it, I thought. Or disappointment. Something.

"Would you like some lemonade? It's pink," she said, and raised an eyebrow.

"Sure, that'd be great," I said. "Thanks."

She took two large glass tumblers decorated with cobalt blue flowers from a cupboard, filled them with lemonade from a pitcher, and placed one in front of me.

"Who have you talked to so far?" she asked as she sat down.

"Well, I talked to Olivia, Haley, and Paul. And Gerry, and Gerry's secretary. And Sharon Falk and her secretary and Bob Hennison's secretary." I decided not to mention Phillip's trio of mistresses, particularly since one of them had once been married to Sue's husband.

Sue gave me a curious look. "Did you have a chance to talk to Anna Schulz?"

I winced. "No," I said. "I was supposed to meet her the morning she died."

She raised her eyebrows at me but didn't say anything.

"I think she knew who killed Phillip," I said. "But she must have decided to blackmail him or something and he killed her."

Sue sighed heavily and shook her head. "That would have been an awfully risky thing to do," she said. "Awfully stupid, to be blunt."

I nodded.

"Have you learned anything from the people you've talked to?"

"Not really," I said. "I'm trying to find out what was going on in his life, but so far all I've learned is that he had a habit of spending time with other women."

Sue rolled her eyes and shook her head a few times. "You sure have that right," she said. "Of course, I don't really know that firsthand, I only heard it from Gerry. Olivia never said a word, and of course Phillip didn't. Personally, I can't understand how two people can live that way."

"So your understanding is that Olivia knew about it?"

She shrugged. "Apparently. That's what Gerry said anyway."

"What did Gerry think of it?"

"Well, he thought it was just appalling. He always said Phil never needed a mid-life crisis because he never got around to leaving adolescence."

I laughed and suddenly wondered if she even knew about Phillip's little fling with Miriam Beechman. "Did he tell you who any of the women were?" I asked.

She frowned and thought for a while. "You know, I don't think he ever mentioned any names. It was always, 'Oh, Phil's at it again, this time it's a secretary or a CPA or a client.' Whatever. I never really paid much attention. I never had much use for Phillip, I'll have to admit. I could never quite see what all the fuss was about. Between you and me, I didn't think he was all that attractive."

"But Gerry looks an awful lot like him, you know."

"Yes, I suppose that's true," she said with a sigh. "But their personalities were so different. If they'd been identical twins, I still would've seen Gerry as attractive and Phil as unattractive. I can't separate looks from character, I never could."

"Yeah, I know what you mean," I said. "Do you know about anything else going on in his life? Anything you think could've gotten him in trouble?"

Sue shook her head. "Nothing comes to mind," she said. "We didn't see all that much of Olivia and Phillip, really. They had their own circle of friends. They'd invite us to parties on occasion, but I always felt it was out of obligation and just about anytime I asked them over, something would come up and they'd cancel at the last minute. I always had the feeling they thought we were beneath them."

"But how could Phillip think that of his own brother?" I said. "And they worked together."

Sue shrugged. "I don't know, it was just a feeling. Maybe I was wrong. Gerry's always telling me I'm paranoid. Maybe he's right."

"Did Gerry and Phillip get along all right?"

"Honestly?" she said. "I think they barely tolerated each other. There was always a tension between them, like a constant rivalry. I noticed it the first time I saw them together and it never really went away."

"Has Gerry ever told you anything about their childhood? Like any big fights between them, or anything like that?"

Sue slowly shook her head. "No, nothing like that.

Gerry doesn't talk much about his childhood. I don't think it was very happy. Their father really was something of a tyrant. He had very strong ideas about how he wanted his children to turn out. They were expected to follow the pattern, fit in with the mold. I don't believe it was ever thought that Phillip or Gerry would be anything but CPAs. I think they both felt that leaving the Big Eight after their dad died was a monumental step toward independence. I suppose it was, for them.''

I sighed. ''Yeah, I suppose so. Well, is there anyone that you can think of who might be able to tell me more?''

''Audrey would be a good one to talk to,'' Sue said. ''She is their sister. She must have some insight into Phillip's personality that the rest of us wouldn't.''

''Okay,'' I said. ''I'll try her next. I really appreciate all the time you've spent with me. If I leave you my number, would you call me if you think of anything else?''

''Oh, certainly,'' Sue said. ''And don't be shy about calling me if you have anymore questions. I'm happy to help.''

Sue walked me to the door and I handed her one of my cards as I was leaving. She waved and gave me a big smile as I drove off. A very nice woman, I thought. Gerry was indeed a lucky guy.

WHEN I GOT HOME, I called Olivia and asked her for Audrey's number. She gave it to me somewhat reluctantly, I thought, and made no attempt at conversation. I thanked her and hung up.

It was almost six, so I made some chicken tacos for supper, thought about feeding Scamper, and then remembered he was gone. I willed myself to think of something else so I thought of Brian, but that was even worse. At seven, I dialed Audrey's number.

"Why don't you come to the house for lunch?" Audrey said when I'd explained my mission. "Say Friday, around noon?"

"That would be great," I said. "Thank you very much."

THE NEXT MORNING, I woke up early and lay in bed for quite a while, trying to remember, without the aid of my file, what I'd discovered so far. Phillip had affairs. Olivia probably knew. They had a lot of money but a good part of it was Olivia's. Unless…Olivia had developed a sudden need for money and she'd used up all of her own. But why? I couldn't see her plugging quarters into a slot machine. Blackmail? Nah.

I really needed to talk to more people. I ran through my mental list. I'd seen Olivia, Paul, Haley, and Peter. Nicole Friedman. Gerry and Sue. I was seeing Audrey on Friday and I hoped to see Bob Hennison the following week. Eunice Waters, Joanne Donnelly, Louise Beaumont. I'd talked only briefly to Sharon Falk but she was getting back to me. Who had I missed? *The receptionist.* I'd never talked to the receptionist.

THIRTEEN

I JUMPED OUT OF BED, got dressed and ate breakfast, drank three cups of tea, and dialed Gerry's firm at nine on the dot.

"Is this the receptionist?" I asked when the receptionist answered. Stupid question, but that's what came out.

"Yes," she said.

I went through the whole story and asked *her* if she'd be willing to talk to me. (Her name is Denise Shaw.) She said certainly she would.

"Do you get a lunch break?" I asked. Another stupid question, but she didn't seem to notice.

"I get from twelve to one, but I have to be back at exactly one."

"Don't worry," I said. "If you can do it today, I can be there before twelve and I probably won't even take up your whole hour. I could take you to lunch and we could talk while we eat. Would that be all right?"

"Sure," she said. "I usually go to The Wells Street Station. Do you know where that is?"

"Sure do," I said. "How about if I meet you there at twelve o'clock? I could even go early and make sure we get a table."

"Good idea," she said. "If you get there early

enough, maybe you can get us one outside next to the river."

"I'll try my best," I said.

That gave me roughly two hours to get something done. I went to the library, said a brief hello to Janice and Emily, and got to work. At eleven-fifteen, I put everything away, had a quick cup of tea, and headed downtown.

The Wells Street Station is on Wells Street (obviously) and abuts the Milwaukee River. I got there at eleven-forty, asked for an outdoor table, and was escorted from the relatively dark interior to a serene and sightly strip along the river's edge. I ordered an iced tea, told them I was waiting for someone, and reveled in the quiet world that seemed so faraway from the noise and bustle of the downtown traffic I'd endured only moments before.

At ten past twelve, the waitress brought Denise and two menus to my table.

"Hi," Denise said with a big smile, and held out her hand. "I'm Denise. I've seen you before when you were in to see Mr. Barry."

I smiled and shook her hand. "Hi, I'm Beth," I said. "I guess I have been sort of a pest over there, huh?"

"Oh, no," she said. "I didn't mean that. I'm sure everyone really appreciates what you're doing." (Now wouldn't that be nice?)

We sat down and chatted about this and that while we looked over our menus. She was about twenty years old, with bright brown eyes and golden blond hair cut in a short, blunt style. She wore sterling silver earrings that dangled when she moved, silver rings on four of her fingers, and some sort of skirt and matching blouse and jacket outfit made from a crepe print material with gold and blue designs.

After the waitress took our orders, Denise looked at me and said, "So what did you want to ask me?"

"Well," I said, "I just want to know if you have any idea at all who killed Phillip Barry or Anna Schulz or if you've ever seen or heard anything suspicious going on in the office."

Denise looked around as if to make sure no one was listening and leaned toward me across the table. "I'll tell you one thing," she whispered. "I'll bet you anything, whoever killed Mr. Barry was the same person who killed Anna."

I raised my eyebrows and gave her a look like I hadn't thought of that myself. "Why do you think that?" I whispered back.

"Because two people don't go getting themselves killed in the same place in two weeks when it's not the same killer, that's why. And besides," she added, after looking around again, "I think Anna knew something about Mr. Barry's death."

"You do?" I said. "Why do you think that?"

"Because I heard her talking to Mr. Barry."

I frowned. "You mean Gerry?"

"Yeah. It was right after Mr. Barry was killed, and she was really upset."

"Are you sure she wasn't just upset because Phillip was dead?" I said.

"No...well, of course, she was really upset about that, too, but she was also upset because of something

else. She was in Mr. Barry's office—Gerry, I mean—
and I could hear her really clearly. She was crying
and everything, and she was all upset, and she said
she was going to the police about Mr. Barry.''

"Did she say anything else? Like what she was
going to tell the police?''

"No. Well, she might have, but I didn't hear the
whole conversation because I was just coming back
from lunch when I heard them talking.''

"Did you hear anything that Gerry said?''

"No,'' she said. "I couldn't hear him at all. They
had the door closed and I just heard her because she
was sort of yelling, you know?''

I nodded. "How long did she stay in there after
you got back?''

Denise shrugged. "Ten minutes, maybe? I didn't
really pay attention. Sorry.''

"That's okay,'' I said. "You're being very helpful.
Did you see Gerry after Anna was in there? Did he
come out of the office at all?''

"Oh, I don't know, I can't remember,'' she said.
"I'm sorry.''

"That's okay, really. You're doing fine.'' I thought
for a moment. "Are you sure it was Gerry she was
talking to?''

Denise creased her forehead. "Well…I guess I just
assumed it was him because they were in his office.''

"So you never actually heard him or saw him?''

"No, I guess I didn't.''

I nodded and thought for a moment.

Denise got a sort of whimsical look on her face.
"Do you think you know who did it?'' she asked.

"No," I said. "I have a few ideas, but not enough to go on for any of them. Do *you* have any other ideas? Did you ever hear anything else, or see anything suspicious going on?"

"Not that I remember," she said.

We finished our lunch and talked about other things until ten minutes to one. I paid the bill and told Denise I'd walk her back to the office. I had a few things I wanted to say to Gerry Barry.

"Just knock on his door," she said when we got there. "I'm sure he'll be glad to see you."

"Okay," I said with a smile. "Thanks, Denise."

"Thanks for the lunch," she said, and smiled back. I nodded and rapped on Gerry's closed door. I heard some movement and then a few moments later, Gerry said, "Yes?"

"It's Beth Hartley," I said. "Are you busy?"

Another hesitation and he opened the door.

"Olivia," I said when I walked inside. "How are you? I'm sorry," I said to both of them. "I didn't know you were busy with someone. I can come back later."

"It's all right, Beth," Olivia said. "I was just leaving."

"You'll take care of that matter?" she said to Gerry.

"You can depend on it," he said in a cheerful voice, but none of the cheerfulness seemed to rub off on her. She left with a sober face and shut the door.

"I'm really sorry," I said. "I'm afraid I interrupted something. I didn't realize there was anyone else in here."

"It's okay," Gerry said with a laugh. "Now, what can I do for you?"

"I just wanted to ask you about Sharon Falk," I said with an apologetic look. "Did you give her a hard time about her affair with Phillip?"

Gerry grinned. "Sharon's a big girl," he said. "You don't need to worry about her."

"Did you tell her that I was the one who told you?"

"No," Gerry said. "And I won't."

"Good," I said with a sigh. "Oh, one more question. Did Anna Schulz ever say anything to you about suspecting anyone or going to the police or anything like that?"

Gerry drew in his breath and slowly let it out, but he didn't say anything.

"She did talk to you, didn't she?" I said.

He pressed his lips together.

"Gerry, please. It's important that I know who she talked to."

He leaned his head against the back of his chair and closed his eyes.

"She talked to me a few days before she was killed," he said in a quiet voice. "I thought she was just being hysterical so I told her to calm down and make sure she knew what she was talking about before she made any wild accusations." He winced and looked a little sick.

"Did she tell you she suspected someone?"

"Yes, but she didn't say whom." He ran his hand through his hair and I saw beads of sweat on his forehead. "I think I talked her out of going to the police," he said. "And she confronted the killer instead." He glanced at me and looked away.

"Oh, Gerry, you can't blame yourself for that. All you did was tell her not to make any unsubstantiated accusations. That was good advice. You certainly didn't tell her to arrange a secret, private meeting with a killer."

"I should've been more receptive," he said. "If I'd only taken her seriously, she might've told me who she suspected and I could've done something."

"Like what?" I said. "Get yourself killed?"

"I don't know," he said, shaking his head. "I don't know."

"This isn't your fault, Gerry, anymore than it's mine."

He gave me a funny look but didn't respond.

"I'll talk to you later, okay?"

He nodded and I let myself out.

THE NEXT DAY was Friday, July 25, the day I met Audrey.

I got up early to get an hour's head start on my work, and quit at eleven-fifteen when I bade everyone adieu and left for the western suburbs.

Audrey Taylor and her husband Richard live in Brookfield, like Gerry and Sue, but in a ritzier and newer section. The house was, in fact, brand new, part of a large subdivision without any trees. Most of the houses didn't even have lawns yet. The Taylor house was all brick, with three stories and Palladian windows in the cathedral-ceilinged foyer. A three-car garage opened on the side and there was a shiny black BMW in the driveway.

Audrey answered the door, dressed in old jeans and a brown T-shirt. Now that was a surprise. "Come in," she said in a polite voice. "We can sit out back on the deck. My housekeeper has made us a salad and iced tea." She smiled a little self-consciously. "I hope you like tuna," she said. "I'm trying to watch my weight."

"Tuna's just fine," I said, trying to look like I meant it. "Thanks."

Audrey is about five-eight, and big-boned, but hardly overweight. She's around forty or so, with short brown hair worn close to her head. Her eyes are blue, like Phillip's and Gerry's, but her face is worn and lined, making her look quite a bit older than her older brothers. She led me through an expansive hall-way, an even more expansive kitchen, and out through sliding doors to an enormous deck with two chaise longues, a large round table with an umbrella, and four chairs.

"This is really nice," I said. "I can see why you like to sit out here."

"I try to spend a little time out here everyday when the weather's nice," she said with a smile. "I do wish we had some trees, though. I can't understand these developers. They buy a tract of land covered with trees and then they cut them all down and leave the homeowners with nothing but bare land. Why can't they build around them?"

"Good question," I said.

We sat at the table in the shade of the umbrella

and moments later, a woman appeared with a tray. The woman smiled pleasantly at me and very warmly at Audrey. "Mimi, this is Beth Hartley," Audrey said. "She's a friend of Peter, Phillip's boy."

"It's nice to meet you, Miss Hartley," Mimi said. "I sure was sorry to hear about Mr. Barry's death."

I smiled and said hello.

"Well, enjoy," Mimi said, after we'd chatted a bit. She went inside and closed the doors behind her.

"She's a wonderful housekeeper," Audrey said, as she put some salad on a plate for me. The salad contained tuna, as promised, along with cherry tomatoes, mushrooms, zucchini, broccoli, and carrots. "I don't know what I'd do without her."

"I feel the same way about mine," I said. "She's like part of my family."

Audrey nodded agreement and poured iced tea into a tall glass garnished with a lemon slice.

"Thank you," I said when she handed it to me. "This is very good," I added, referring to the salad (and I meant it).

"Mimi's salads are the best," Audrey said.

We ate for a while in silence, enjoying the warm breeze and the few birds who came near despite the absence of trees.

"I understand it was Peter who asked you to help solve Phillip's murder," she said a bit later. "He's told me a lot about you. He's very fond of you, but I'm sure you already know that."

I nodded and smiled. "I'm very fond of him, too," I said. "He seemed to think you might be able to help. In fact, Sue said the same thing."

Audrey frowned and looked a little confused. "I'm not sure how," she said. "Phillip was my brother, of course, but I knew very little of what went on in his life. Especially after we grew up. We really led very separate lives."

"What about as a child?" I said. "Can you tell me what he was like then?"

Audrey took a deep breath and let it out, then looked off in the distance for sometime. "Well," she finally said, "I think the best way to sum Phillip up is to say he was complex. And mysterious. Very secretive. Whenever I thought I had him pegged he'd turn around and do something that completely surprised me."

"Like what?" I said.

"Phillip was the type—at least I thought he was the type—that followed all the rules. He never drove over the speed limit, he never cheated in school, he always came home when he was supposed to. Everything by the book. But then, when he was seventeen, he had an affair with one of my mother's married friends. It was a complete shock to everyone. Entirely out of character. My mother never said a word to my father about it. I think he would've killed him if he knew."

"Did the woman's husband know?"

"Yes, he did. He almost killed Phillip himself."

I raised my eyebrows.

Audrey gave me a little smile. "That was almost thirty years ago. He wouldn't have killed him for it *now*."

"No, I suppose not," I said.

Mimi came back just then, to retrieve the tray and ask if we wanted anything else. "Are there any of those brownies left?" Audrey asked with a mischievous look.

"Now Ms. Taylor, you know what you told me."

"Oh, I've been good all day," Audrey said. "Just bring us two, and two cups of coffee?" she said as she gave me a questioning look.

"Sure," I said with a grin.

"Okay," Mimi said, "but don't say I didn't try."

Audrey laughed when Mimi'd gotten inside. "I've recruited her to help me diet, but I'm afraid I resist all her help."

I laughed along with her. "You said Phillip was mysterious and secretive," I said then. "What did you mean by that?"

"Well, he was secretive about the affair, for one. We found out about that from the woman's husband. And then there was the time he was planning to go to law school instead of joining Arthur Andersen. He'd actually been accepted at Berkeley and UW but Father found out and put an end to the whole thing. I don't think Phillip ever forgave him for that."

"When did your father die?" I said.

"Ten years ago. My mother died three years after that."

"I'm sorry," I said. "I feel pretty lucky that both my parents are still alive."

Audrey nodded, but I had the impression she didn't share my sentiment.

Mimi came out again, with two brownies and two cups of coffee, a pitcher of cream, and a jar of artificial sweetener. "I'll be taking off in a minute," Mimi said to Audrey. "Say hello to Chocolate for me."

Audrey grinned. "I surely will," she said. "Thank you, Mimi. I'll see you tomorrow."

"See you tomorrow," Mimi said back and gave me a friendly nod and a smile.

"Chocolate?" I said to Audrey after Mimi had left.

"My horse," Audrey said. "He's all brown, like a big chocolate bar. Do you ride?"

"No," I said. "But I had a friend in high school who had a horse and I went riding with her a few times. She always rode bareback, though, and it really hurt the next day."

"Oh, my," Audrey said. "I'll bet it did. I try to spend some time with Chocolate at least three times a week. We're still getting to know each other. A horse can be good company when you get to be friends."

"Did you have horses when you were young?"

Audrey nodded. "I was given a mare for my seventh birthday. I named her Candy."

I laughed. "I think there's a pattern here."

"Yes, I'm afraid so. Horses and sweets, my two biggest weaknesses."

"Tell me about your children," I said. "Peter said you have two boys."

"Yes, Rich and Steven." Audrey smiled with the left side of her mouth. "They're the image of their father. Already being groomed for the law and barely in high school."

"You're husband's a lawyer?"

"Yes," Audrey said with a sigh. "I rarely see him, he's so busy. I suppose the same will be true of my boys before long."

She had a very sad and lonely look on her face.

"What's your horse like?" I asked, hoping to get her mind on a happier topic. Her face brightened immediately.

"Frisky as can be," she said with a big smile, and went on to tell me horse tale after horse tale for the next fifteen minutes.

"I'm afraid I haven't been much help to you," she said later. "Phillip told me very little about his personal or business life. We didn't see much of each other or even talk much, although we lived in the same city." She sighed with a pained look on her face. "I should've tried harder, I suppose, and now it's too late." She looked up at me and I gave her a sympathetic smile. "I know this is a terrible thing to say," she said, watching my face for a reaction, "but I almost feel angry with Phillip for getting killed. I'm angry that he never bothered to know me or be a part of my life, because he got himself killed and closed off all the possibilities. Isn't that ridiculous?"

"No, not really," I said. "I can understand your feeling that way. I think people are often angry when someone dies and there's unfinished business between them. It's like you're saying, 'Why did you waste all of our lives and not pay any attention to me or get close to me and now you're dead and it's too late?'

Audrey smiled at me with moist eyes. She started

to say something but was fighting back her tears, so she squeezed my hand instead.

I managed, a few minutes later, to get her talking about Chocolate again, and her mood improved considerably.

"Do you have anymore questions about Phillip?" she asked a bit later. "I'm afraid I haven't been much help."

"No, you have, really. You've given me some insight into his personality that I didn't really have before."

She seemed pleased at that.

"How did he and Gerry get along when they were children?" I asked.

Audrey laughed. "They were at each other's throats constantly," she said. "Who was going to impress Father the most? Who would best live up to all his expectations?" She shook her head. "You know, I see the same thing in my boys. They live to please their father. I give them all the love and acceptance they could possibly want, and all they think about is, does it please Richard? It was the same thing with Phillip and Gerry. My mother would have loved them no matter what they did, but they never seemed to care. It was as if she wasn't even there. They lived only to please my father, who, for the most part, was impossible to please. I thought the rivalry between them had ended when they went into business together, but from what I could see, it only got worse."

I frowned. "Really?" I said.

She just shrugged in response.

"Well, I suppose it's pretty hard to break lifelong habits."

"Yes," Audrey said. She checked her watch and flashed me a guilty look. "I hate to cut this short," she said, "but if I don't get going I won't get much of a ride in. You're welcome to come with me and meet Chocolate. There are other horses, if you'd like to ride with me."

I smiled. "Maybe some other time," I said. "I'm a little behind on my work from all this investigating and I'd really better get back to it."

Audrey smiled, too, but looked disappointed, and I felt bad. "I promise I'll take a rain check, though," I said.

"Wonderful," she said with a big grin.

When I got home, I made a few notes about my meeting with Audrey, added a reminder to make sure I took her up on her horseback-riding invitation, and went to the library.

"Learn anything?" Emily said when I came in.

"Not really," I said with a despondent look. "I need more information but I've run out of people to talk to. I've interviewed everyone in his family and everyone currently available at the firm. Who else is there?"

"Didn't he have any friends?" Janice said.

I stared at her. How stupid could I be?

"I'll be back," I said.

FOURTEEN

I WENT TO THE KITCHEN and dialed Olivia's number.

"There's Tom Hanson," she said in response to my question. "He was at the funeral. Hold on and I'll get you his number."

I waited, and marveled at how friendly and cooperative she was being *this time*.

In a few moments she was back, and she gave me the man's home and business numbers. "Were they business acquaintances or just friends?" I asked her.

"I think they may have met through business, but they were friends for years. They played racquetball every Tuesday morning for as long as I can remember."

"Okay, thanks, Olivia."

After I hung up, I called Gerry and asked him the same question. He gave me the same name, and one other. "Sam Goldstein," he said. "We grew up together. He and Phillip have always kept in touch."

"Does he still live in Milwaukee?"

"As far as I know. He had a big mansion in Whitefish Bay and he owns a chain of hardware stores. I doubt if he's moved."

I thanked Gerry, too, and hung up.

Well, who would it be, Tom Hanson or Sam Goldstein? I tried Tom Hanson first since I already had his numbers.

No one answered at the home number and I decided not to leave a message for the time being. I tried the business number next.

A receptionist answered, said something I didn't understand, and waited for me to speak. I asked for Tom Hanson.

"Can you hold, please?" she said.

"Tom Hanson," a gruff voice said.

"Mr. Hanson," I said. "I'm sorry to bother you at work. I'm a friend of the Phillip Barry family and I'm helping investigate his death. I understand you were a good friend of his and I was hoping I could talk to you about him."

After a slight hesitation, he said, "I'm not sure I understand. Are you with the police?"

I explained.

Another hesitation. "Sure, I'll talk to you," he said. "But this isn't a good time. I'm going to be tied up here until about six-thirty. I could meet you somewhere after that."

"Sure, that'd be great," I said.

He told me where he was, which was downtown. I suggested coffee or a drink, but he all but insisted we go to dinner at Café Marché in the Third Ward. "I've had a craving all day for their Pecan Turtle Tart," he said. "If I don't get my weekly fix I start to go into withdrawal."

I laughed. "Okay," I said. "You talked me into it."

We exchanged descriptions, chatted another minute, and agreed to meet there at seven o'clock.

When Janice and Emily went home at five, I

brought my Phillip file into the kitchen, made myself a cup of tea, and tried to think of everything and anything I might want to ask Tom Hanson.

At six o'clock, I took a shower, put on a pale pink cotton dress, piled my hair on top of my head, and headed for the Third Ward.

Milwaukee's historic Third Ward is the city's former wholesaling and manufacturing district, gloriously revitalized in the 1980s. It was nothing but vacant warehouses for twenty years, but now it's full of life, housing antiques and boutiques, jewelry stores, art, theater, comedy and restaurants, as well as residences. I've heard it's a wonderful place to live.

It's certainly a wonderful place to take a walk.

I found a parking space very near the restaurant and was about to walk in when a man standing outside the door caught my attention.

"Are you Beth?" he asked a little shyly.

I nodded and smiled. "Tom?"

He was about five-ten, a little stocky but well built from what I could see, straight brown hair, and a really full brown moustache flecked with gray.

His eyes were big and brown. I guessed him to be in his late forties or early fifties. He was wearing a suit but he'd removed the jacket and loosened his tie.

We went in and made somewhat self-conscious small talk until we were shown to our table (a matter of two minutes), and then busied ourselves with the menus until the waitress came for our drink order. For some reason, he made me nervous, and I think I was having the same effect on him.

"So," he said, when the waitress left, "tell me again how you got involved in this thing."

"Phillip's son, Peter, shovels my walk in the winter—they live down the block from me—and we're pretty close. Last year, my secretary's younger brother was murdered and she asked me to help her prove it because it was made to look like a suicide and she was afraid the police wouldn't take it seriously. So I said yes and then I did."

"You did what?"

"I proved it."

His eyes widened and he gave me an amazed smile. "You mean you really solved the murder?" he said.

"Yeah, I really did."

"Wow, that's quite an accomplishment. Did they give you an award for that?"

I grinned. "No, but I think they were grateful. Well, sort of."

Tom laughed. "Well, I should certainly hope so," he said. I couldn't believe it. He was truly impressed. No one else had ever reacted that way.

"So, anyway," I said, "Peter knew I'd solved that murder so he asked me to help investigate his father's murder. I tried to talk him out of it but he was so insistent and I just couldn't say no."

Tom nodded. "Well. I think Peter's very lucky to have you for a friend. It must be dangerous work at times."

"Yeah, it can be."

"So, how can I help?" he said.

"Well, you and Phillip were pretty good friends, right?"

He nodded. ''We got together at least once a week for racquetball. Drinks, now and then.''

''Did he talk to you about his personal life?''

Tom stiffened a little and frowned. ''Some,'' he said.

''Did he ever talk to you about Olivia or the women he had affairs with?''

Now he shifted in his seat and loosened his tie a bit more. ''He didn't talk about Olivia much,'' he said.

''How about the other women?''

Tom puffed out his cheeks and looked at me.

''You're not comfortable talking about this, are you?''

His shoulders relaxed and he gave me a sheepish grin. ''No,'' he said. ''I'm not.''

''I'm sorry,'' I said. ''I know it seems like you're betraying a confidence but it's only in the interest of helping to find Phillip's killer. I think he'd forgive you on that account.'' I gave him an entreating smile.

He smiled back and sighed. ''I guess you're right,'' he said. ''It wasn't that much of a secret to begin with,'' he added with a laugh.

''You mean Olivia knew?''

Tom raised his eyebrows and gave a little shrug. ''I don't see how she couldn't have,'' he said.

''Why do you say that?''

''Because he did it so often, for one thing, and for such extended periods of time. He'd take off entire weekends sometimes and he'd do it for three or four months in a row. How could she not know?''

"Yeah, I see what you mean. Was he ever serious about any of these women?"

Tom thought for a moment before he answered. "For the most part, I'd have to say no," he said. "But there were a few I think he took more seriously."

"Do you know who they were?"

"Well, there was a secretary some years back. Pat something or other."

"Patricia Morgan?" I said.

"That's the name."

"Anyone else?"

"One of his accountants, a woman named Sharon Falk, I believe."

"What makes you think he took them more seriously than the others?"

"They lasted longer, for one thing. And he talked about them differently."

"Do you know why he stopped seeing them?"

Tom shrugged. "Phillip never wanted to talk about the ending of a relationship. He'd say it was history. Over and done with, so why discuss it? But my guess is...do you want me to guess?"

I grinned and nodded.

He gave me a smile that lasted a few moments. "My guess is they started to complain that he didn't spend enough time with them, or they were expecting too much. Like him getting a divorce, for instance."

"So you don't think he ever contemplated leaving Olivia for one of them?"

"Never," Tom said. "Why would he? He had everything he wanted. If he got divorced, he'd have lost half of it. More than half."

"Do you think either of those women could have been bitter enough about his leaving them that they might kill him for it?"

He gave me one of those "Oh, come on" looks. "No," he said as he shook his head. "I can't see that at all. Phillip never gave them any false hopes. He'd tell them right up front that he was married and he wasn't getting divorced. You'd think that'd scare them off, but it rarely did. Believe it or not, it actually seemed to heighten their interest. I used to tell him he had better luck with women as a married man than I had as a divorced one."

The waitress arrived with our dinners just then (roasted duck with sauerkraut, carrots, and caramelized rutabagas for me—*absolutely marvelous*—and veal Marsala for him). We chatted about other things for a while, and then I moved the conversation back to Phillip.

"What about his business?" I said. "Did he ever talk about that?"

"Nothing specific," Tom said. "He'd give me information sometimes that he thought would benefit me in my business, but he never discussed any business he had with clients. It's not something I'd expect him to do."

"Did he ever mention receiving any threats of any kind or being afraid of someone? Anything like that?"

Tom shook his head. "No, never. And I saw him the day before he died. He was fine. Acted like he always did. I didn't get the idea anything was worrying him."

I sat back in my chair with a defeated look on my face.

He smiled. "It's not easy coming up with an answer, is it?"

"No," I said. "It sure isn't."

"You seem to be going at it the right way, though," he said with an encouraging look. "I have a feeling you're going to crack this thing. Just give it time."

"Thanks," I said with a smile. "Do you have any ideas at all about who killed him?"

Tom shook his head a few times. "Not a one," he said. Then he wrinkled his brow. "His secretary was killed, too. What do you make of that?"

"I think she knew who killed Phillip," I said. "And I think she confronted the killer."

Tom raised his eyebrows and let out a deep breath. He had a thoughtful look on his face, so I waited.

"Maybe it was related to the business," he said. "His secretary might be in a position to know about it if it had something to do with the firm."

"Yeah, that's true," I said. "Peter got me thinking it might be a client. Like someone who was doing something illegal that Phillip found out about and they killed him to keep him quiet."

"There you go," Tom said. "That certainly sounds plausible."

We shifted the topic, then, to my business (which he seemed genuinely interested in) and his (he's an insurance adjuster). Then the waitress brought us our dessert.

"You have to try some of this," Tom said. "I think I'm addicted to this stuff."

I laughed, and he handed me a spoonful of chocolate butter cream, chopped pecans, and caramel sauce.

"Oh, my gosh, this is great," I said. "I want more."

He laughed (a really wonderful, deep laugh, by the way), and gave me another spoonful. We stayed maybe half an hour more, taking time with our after-dinner coffee, and then we went home.

I hated to admit it, but I *really* liked him a lot.

THE REST OF THE WEEKEND was relatively unproductive, Phillip-wise, though I'd more than make up for it on Monday. I got up early on Saturday morning, made some lemon and poppy seed muffins for breakfast, and then spent an hour and a half grocery shopping. After I put everything away, which took another half hour, I did whatever precooking I could of the dinner I was bringing to Mrs. Robinson's the next day. This time, it was chicken cacciatore, biscuits, as always, a salad with homemade Italian dressing, some olives, and a little blue cheese, and pound cake with blueberries, strawberries, slivered almonds, and whipped cream for dessert. I precooked the chicken cacciatore (except for the pasta, of course), put the cake in the oven, and went out on the screened porch with a cup of tea and another muffin.

I whiled away the day doing a little work now and then, a little reading, a little sewing, even some knitting. Brian didn't call, which was no surprise, and I didn't call him either. I tried Sam Goldstein at three, but a woman answered and said he was out. I told her what I wanted (after learning she was his wife), and asked her to have him call me. She said she would.

I had an appointment to get my hair cut, ran my car through a car wash after that, and had a message from Sam Goldstein when I got back. I returned the call, praying he'd still be home, and I was in luck.

I introduced myself, went through my preliminary explanation, and asked if he'd mind discussing Phillip with me.

He hesitated a moment. "I don't know what I can tell you," he said. "I sure don't have any idea who killed him."

"Well, maybe you can tell me something about him that you wouldn't necessarily realize was important, but that might give me a clue as to what happened."

Another hesitation. "Well, I don't know what that could be but I can give it a shot. What'd you have in mind?"

"Would you like to meet me somewhere so we could talk?" I said.

"If it's all the same to you," he said, "I'd rather do it now, over the phone. I don't mean to be rude, but I don't have a lot of free time."

"That's fine," I said. "I'll try to keep it short. When was the last time you saw Phillip?"

"About two weeks before he died. We met for a drink."

"Was there some special reason for getting together?"

"No, we did that occasionally, just to keep in touch."

"Did he talk about any trouble he might have been having with anyone?"

"No, nothing like that," Sam said. "Tell you the truth, he was mostly complaining about the Brewers."

I laughed. "So he was just his usual self? Nothing seemed to be bothering him?"

"Nothing out of the ordinary, no."

"What do you mean by 'the ordinary'?" I said. "Did he have some sort of ongoing problem that was always on his mind?"

"No more than the rest of us," Sam said, but this time he sounded a little impatient. "He had the same complaints as all of us. Business, the wife, you know."

"Did he complain much about his wife?"

Sam sighed. "Look," he said. "I'm not sure where you're going with this, but I don't really feel comfortable repeating everything he told me, okay?"

"I'm sorry," I said. "I know it sounds like I'm just being nosy, but I'm trying to learn as much as I can about him so I can figure out what happened. If I don't know what was going on with him, I won't get anywhere."

I heard him sigh again. "Yeah, I hear you," he said. "Okay, listen. Yeah, he talked a lot about Olivia. And he talked a lot about a whole lot of other women, too, okay? He and Olivia had what you might call an understanding, only she hadn't been so understanding lately.''

"How so?" I said.

"He had something going with someone sometime back and Olivia got all hot about it. Ever since then, she wasn't so understanding, know what I mean?"

"Did he tell you who the woman was?"

Sam laughed. "He had so many coming and going I couldn't keep track. I can't give you a name. Sorry."

"Do you remember when that was?" I asked.

"Oh, geez. Well, it must have been sometime in the fall, because we were at a football game when he told me about it."

"Do you know if he was seeing anyone currently?"

"I don't think so," Sam said. "He never mentioned anyone."

"Did he ever talk to you about any problems he had with clients, or anyone else? Even sometime way in the past. Anything you can think of."

Sam thought for a few moments. "Naw, I can't think of anything."

"Okay," I said. "I really appreciate your talking to me. I hope I didn't take up too much of your time."

"No problem," he said.

I gave him my number in case he should think of anything else, and hung up.

I CALLED EMILY a little later and asked her if she wanted to see a movie since Phil was out of town, but we couldn't find one we could agree on. She came over instead, and we watched videos (two Woody Allen movies), ate popcorn, and talked—mostly about Phil, and a little about Brian.

"Maybe I should just divorce him," she said, "while I'm still young enough to find someone else."

I frowned and gave her a skeptical look. "Is there anything about your relationship with Phil that you think wouldn't occur if you were with someone else?" I said.

She wrinkled her brow.

"What I mean is, do you think your problems with Phil are caused by something peculiar to Phil, something about *him* that makes you incompatible, or do you think you would feel the same way with anyone?"

Emily put a bit of a sneer on her face. "What kind of a question is that?" she said. "You're making it sound like it's all me and not him. You always do that."

"No, I don't," I said. "I'm not trying to say it's your fault. I'm just trying to get you to think about why you feel it's not working. I don't want you to end up ruining your whole life for the wrong reasons. What if you divorced Phil, married someone else, and the same thing happened all over again? You would've lost Phil and you wouldn't be any better off."

"Well, I wouldn't be any worse off, either."

"You would be if no one else turned out to be as patient and understanding as Phil is, and if no one else loved you the way he does."

Emily's face clouded up and her eyes suddenly

filled with tears. She opened her mouth to say something and closed it again.

"I'm not saying you're not worthy of being loved by someone else," I said gently. "Anyone would be extremely lucky to have you. But you are very complicated and hard to understand, especially to *men*, who never understand *anything*. And Phil knows what you're like and he loves you for who you are. I think you're unhappy despite Phil, not because of him. I can't even stand to think how miserable you'd be if you really lost him."

"Well, then why am I so miserable now?" she said.

"I don't know," I said. "Sometimes I think you're just chronically unhappy. It's like there's something you want, like there's always something missing from your life, but you have no idea what it is."

Emily put her face in her hands.

"Maybe it's just part of your personality and you're going to be that way forever, no matter what."

She lifted her head and gaped at me. "Well, thanks a lot," she said. "Is that supposed to make me feel better, or what?"

I gave her a guilty look. "Sorry," I said. "It's just that you've been going through the same thing over and over since we were twelve years old. It's like you're in a perpetual mid-life crisis. I don't think it has anything to do with Phil. You were like this before you met him. He's probably the only stability you have."

"What makes you such an expert?"

"I'm not. I'm just telling you what I think is

wrong, based on my knowing you for all these years. I know I could be wrong, it's just what I think.''

"Well, you are wrong," Emily said. "So just drop it.''

We did, and moved on to Brian. Then she tried to tell me what my problems were. I didn't mention Tom Hanson even once. I was so proud of myself.

I WOKE UP very tired the next day. I was just finishing my very late breakfast, when my mom called.

"Well, I suppose you're having dinner with that woman again," she said.

"Mom," I said. "Her name is Mrs. Robinson. You would love her. She's a very nice person."

"I'm sure she is," Mom said. "But it would be nice if you'd have Sunday dinner with your family once in a while. You used to come every week."

"I know," I said. "But we stopped doing that a long time ago because Dad wasn't there half the time. He always had those meetings."

"Just the same," my mother said.

I sighed. "Mom, I come over a lot during the day on Sundays. I was even planning to come today. Do you want me to?"

"Of course I want you to," she said. "I always want you to."

"Great. I'll be there in half an hour."

My mom and dad live in the city of Wauwatosa, in an old, established, tree-lined neighborhood. The house is all brick with hunter green shutters (real ones) and a dark red door. There are pale pink gardenias in the window boxes and even paler pink roses forming an arch over the front door. They have screen doors in front and back so they can leave the other doors open in summer and early fall. When I walked in, my mom and dad were moving one of the living room couches, and all the other furniture was in the middle of the room.

"What are you doing?" I said.

"Rearranging the furniture," my dad said. "How does it look?"

"Very funny," I said. "Want some help?"

The answer was yes, so I spent the next half hour moving and re-moving furniture. When we were through, I looked around.

"Mom, isn't this the way it was before?"

"No," she said. "That table used to be where this one is."

I rolled my eyes.

My mother went into the kitchen and I followed. "I have some coffee cake," she said, "and there's a fresh pot of coffee."

"Ooh, great," I said. I cut myself a small piece of cake, poured a cup of coffee, and sat down at the kitchen table. My dad came in a minute later and did the same.

"How's the boy doing?" my dad said.

I wrinkled my brow. "You mean Peter?"

"Mm, hmm," Dad said with his mouth full.

"He's doing okay," I said. "Although he got pretty frantic when the secretary was killed."

"*What?*" my mom said. My dad almost choked on his cake. I was sure they'd have heard about it on the news.

"The father's secretary?" my dad said, when he'd recovered.

"Yeah, her name was Anna Schulz. I think she knew who Phillip Barry's killer was and she tried to blackmail him or something and then he killed her, too."

"You'd better stay out of this, Beth," my mom said. "This is too dangerous."

"Mom, I'm not going to get hurt. I wouldn't be stupid enough to try to blackmail a killer. That's probably what got her killed, you know."

My father took a deep breath, and let it out. "What your mother means," he said "is that this man, or woman for that matter, has killed two people already, and there is no reason to believe he wouldn't kill you, too, if you got in his way. Now, I know you don't like to be told what to do, so I'm not telling you, I'm asking you. Would you please let the police handle this, for our sakes if not your own?"

I sighed. "I'm not really doing all that much, Dad. It's Brian's case this time and he's working really hard on it. I'm sure he'll figure it out very quickly."

They both looked relieved. They've always been easy to fool. "Okay," my dad said. "You just be careful and let Brian do the dirty work."

"Don't worry, Dad," I said.

I stayed until two and then went back to my house to get ready to go to Mrs. Robinson's. I stayed *there* until eight, went home and NordicTracked for a bit, and went to bed. I didn't know it then, but tomorrow would prove to be an interesting day.

FIFTEEN

I GOT UP AT SEVEN on Monday morning, worked until ten, delivered a brief, and worked some more. Louise Beaumont called at twelve-fifteen.

"Mr. Hennison can spare five minutes for you at precisely three o'clock this afternoon," she said.

"Great," I said. "I'll be there."

We had another brief-frenzy going so we ordered Chinese for lunch, worked while we ate, and at *precisely* two-thirty, I left to keep my appointment with Mr. Hennison.

I was ushered in as soon as I arrived, told to sit, and subjected to a penetrating stare. Bob Hennison was bald, probably fifty or fifty-five, with pale blue eyes and wire-rimmed glasses.

"Miss Hartley, how can I help you?" he said without smiling.

"How well did you know Phillip Barry?" I said. It was an abrupt start, but I only had four and a half minutes left.

"We were acquainted professionally, not personally." He spoke rapidly, but very precisely, in a clipped sort of way. It made me nervous.

"Was he in any kind of trouble that you know of?"

"None that I'm aware of."

"Why didn't you come back for the funeral?"

That question seemed to unnerve him a bit. He shifted in his seat and hesitated before he answered. "It couldn't be helped," he said in a near-normal voice. "I had two very important papers to present, both of which involved a great deal of preparation, much of which was Phillip's. We'd worked on them together for over fourteen months. It may appear harsh, Miss Hartley, but Phillip would have wanted me to stay."

I gave him a weak smile and nodded. "I'm sure you're right," I said. "I don't suppose you have any idea who might have killed him?"

"No, I'm afraid not," he said. Then he stood and offered me his hand. "I hope you'll forgive me, but I have a client waiting. I'm sorry I can't help you."

"That's okay," I said. "Thank you for your time."

JANICE AND EM were still plugging away when I got back home. They both stayed pretty late, so we ordered pizza for dinner and kept right on going. At eight-fifteen, after they'd both gone home, I got a phone call from Joanne Donnelly, Gerry's secretary.

"I found something that might help solve the case," she said excitedly.

Now, that got my attention. "Where are you?" I said.

"At home, but I found something in one of the files. You *have* to see this."

"What is it?" I said.

"It's a letter from Mr. Barry to one of his clients, and it says he knows all about this guy selling stolen goods and embezzling and a whole bunch of other illegal stuff. Mr. Barry was going to turn him in if he didn't do it himself.''

"Oh, my gosh," I said. "You're talking about Phillip, right?"

"Right," she said. "I just know this has to be it. It's just like you said. He killed Mr. Barry to keep him from turning him in."

This was almost too good to be true. "What's the client's name?" I said.

"Adrian Adrian," Joanne said. "The name of the business is Adrian, Adrian and Adrian."

"Did it have a date on it?"

"Uh...I think it was about three weeks ago," she said. "That's a pretty good motive for murder, isn't it?"

"Yeah," I said. "It sure is. Where did you find it?"

"In Mrs. Falk's office. All of Mr. Barry's files are in there and she's out of town so I knew I wouldn't get caught."

"This is great," I said. "Would you mind if I came over and got it?"

Slight hesitation. "I don't have it," she said. "I thought I heard someone coming so I was afraid to take it out of the file. I'm sorry, I'll get it tomorrow, I promise."

"No," I said quickly. "Don't do that. I don't want you taking anymore chances. I'll do it."

"*You* will?" she said. "But how will you get in?"

"You could let me in?" I said in a plaintive voice.

Joanne gasped. "I can't do that," she said. "I could get in a lot of trouble for that."

"Yes, but you could also get in a lot of trouble if you get caught searching the files yourself. Besides, you can let me in and then leave. If someone catches me, I won't tell them who let me in."

"Oh, I don't know," she said.

"Please," I said. "We could really be on to something. You don't want to just forget about it, do you?"

She let out a whine. "No, I guess not," she said. "Okay, I'll let you in, but you have to swear you'll never tell."

"Don't worry," I said. "I won't. How did you manage to stay after everyone was gone?"

"I do that a lot. I can't always get my work done during office hours so I have to stay late."

"Okay," I said. "What time does everyone usually leave?"

"Well, it varies, but usually everyone's gone by seven or eight. Tonight it was seven."

"Okay, I'll tell you what. Tomorrow night, I'll wait for you to call me after everyone's gone and then I'll come over and you can let me in."

More whining.

"And then you can go home," I said. "Don't worry, no one's going to catch me. Why would they come back after they'd already left?"

"Okay," she said with a groan.

THE NEXT DAY went by so slowly I could have screamed. I was nervous to start with about searching Phillip's files, but the more I thought about it, the crazier I thought I was for even contemplating such a thing. On the other hand, I told myself, how can I expect to solve a murder if I'm going to be a little wimp whenever something like this comes up? What was I supposed to do, go running to Brian every time things got a little difficult? There was no way I was going to do that. So that settled it, I was going through with the plan. Besides, I had every intention of looking for more than just the letter to Adrian Adrian. What I really wanted was a chance to search Gerry's office.

At 8:10 p.m., Joanne called.

"They're gone," she whispered. "Please hurry up, I'm dying in here."

"Just hang on," I said. "I'll be right there."

AT 8:25, I WAS IN the building and I'd sent Joanne home. I left all the lights on so things wouldn't look suspicious and went right for Sharon's office and closed the door.

The room was a disaster. There were files and papers everywhere and I didn't really know where to start. Nothing was organized in any discernible fashion. I should've asked Joanne where the Adrian file was, but it was too late now.

I started with the chair behind the desk and carefully lifted the corner of every file so as not to disturb the "order" in which Sharon had left them. No luck.

I tried the desk next, which presented more of a challenge since everything was piled in what appeared to be a haphazard manner, files on top of files, laid every which way. After more than ten minutes, I decided to abandon the desk for the time being and try something else. It seemed unlikely that Joanne had found Adrian's file on the bottom of that mess.

I went for one of the two chairs in front of the desk next, and followed my same careful method. As I was lifting the corner of the last file in that pile, I heard someone come in and I knocked everything to the floor. I tried to pick the papers up, but I heard footsteps approaching so I left everything where it was and looked around frantically for a place to hide. No closets, no other exits, nothing! I ran around and crouched down behind the desk.

A moment later, the door opened. I could hear whomever it was picking up the files I'd dropped on the floor and putting them back on the chair. A few moments later, I heard a vacuum cleaner.

I very gingerly peeked out from behind the desk and saw a woman with her back to me, vacuuming the floor. I let out a loud sigh, which she didn't hear, quietly removed the files from the desk chair, sat down at the desk, and pretended to work. When she finally turned around and saw me, she let out a scream and jumped about two feet. I frowned at her and waited for her to turn off her machine.

"You give me quite a fright," she said with a heavy accent. "I do not see you when I come in. Lordy, Lord," she said, and patted her chest.

"I'm sorry," I said. "I didn't mean to frighten you. I was just looking for something under the desk."

"I come back later, when you are done working," she said.

"Thank you," I said with a smile. "I won't be long."

She appeared to believe I belonged there, so I waited until she left and closed the door, and resumed my search. For some reason, knowing she was out there actually made me feel more secure, though it pretty much destroyed my plans to look through Gerry's office.

I started on the second chair, this time taking less trouble to leave things as I'd found them (after all, it was starting to feel like my office). Still no luck, though. My next target was the couch. Five neatly stacked piles, which made it easier, and Adrian's file was right on top of the second pile I searched.

I found the letter, removed it, and carefully looked through everything else, not really expecting to find anything more incriminating than that. And I didn't. I found a lot of financial statements and other accounting type things, but no additional reference to any illegal activity. I went out of Sharon's office, letter in hand, smiled at the cleaning woman, and wandered around trying to look like I knew what I was doing, until I found a copy machine. I turned it on, waited what seemed like an hour for it to warm up, copied the letter, and went back to Sharon's office. I closed the door, put the original letter back in the file, took a quick look around to make sure I'd left things in the disarray I'd found them, and left.

I CALLED JOANNE as soon as I got home. "I got it," I said. "And I didn't get caught."

"Thank goodness," she said. "Do you really think he did it?"

"Well, I don't know," I said. "But he certainly had a motive."

After I hung up, I thought about calling Brian, but I didn't. Not yet. I wanted to be a little more certain before I made a fool of myself. I wanted to pay Mr. Adrian Adrian a visit, first.

THE NEXT DAY was busy, as usual, but I was preoccupied. As hard as I tried, I couldn't get Adrian Adrian off my mind.

When we broke for lunch, I looked through the yellow pages for his business—and found it. Adrian, Adrian and Adrian, on Forest Home Avenue, right off of Forty-third Street. I dialed the number and asked how late they were open. "Eight p.m.," the man said. Perfect. I'd take a ride out after work.

"This is getting more intriguing by the minute," I said to Janice and Emily in a teasing voice. "I'm going to go see a guy named Adrian Adrian tonight."

"Who is he?" Emily said.

"One of Phillip's clients. Phillip wrote him a letter and threatened to turn him in for embezzlement and a few other things."

Emily looked impressed (really). "How'd you find that out?" she said.

"I searched the files," I said, very nonchalantly.

She smiled and then laughed. "You have a lot of guts," she said.

"Thanks," I said with a look of surprise, and Janice winked at me.

We worked until five, I ate a quick dinner of yogurt and a banana, and then headed for Adrian, Adrian and Adrian.

Forest Home Avenue, near Forty-third, is an area I'm familiar with from my childhood. It's right near Jackson Park and the Kinnickinnic River Parkway. *I should've planned this out ahead of time,* I was thinking on my drive over. *I don't know what makes me think this guy is going to be willing to talk to me.* I decided to take a ride through the park, first, until I decided on my approach.

The park was full of people picnicking, feeding ducks, swimming in the pool, or just walking or lying on the grass. I had to pay too much attention to the pedestrians to be able to think, so I pulled over to the side when I found a free spot and turned off the engine. I opened the notebook I brought with me, got out my pen, and started doodling. Five little duckies later, I had it. I'd just tell the guy I was a close friend of the family and that someone had told me he and Phillip were good friends and that he might be willing to help me. That ought to catch him off guard. Then again, it might just make him angry. I'd soon find out.

"Is Adrian Adrian here?" I said in a sweet voice to the man behind the counter. The guy was no more than five-five, probably two hundred pounds, with a greasy bald head with a little string of black hair that stretched from one side of his head to the other, a dirty face, and dirty fingernails. He wore a black T-shirt with "Harley-Davidson" on the front and blue-jean cutoffs that showed off his lovely legs.

"Who wants to know?" he said. He had a toothpick in his mouth and he chewed on it, gave me a little leering smile, and eyed me up and down, all at the same time. Very coordinated.

I smiled as innocently as I could and said, "My name is Beth Hartley. I'm a friend of a friend of Mr. Adrian."

He wrinkled his brow. "What friend is that?" he said.

"Phillip Barry."

He shifted his position and looked into my eyes with a cold stare.

"Are you Mr. Adrian?" I said.

"Barry's dead," he said. "What do you want to talk to me for?"

"So you are Adrian Adrian."

"Yeah, yeah, I'm Adrian," he said.

"I'm a good friend of the family," I said, "and I'm helping to investigate Phillip's murder. I was told that you were a good friend of his and that you might be willing to help."

He put the toothpick back in his mouth and did the

same leering and chewing act again. "A lady detective, well, what do you know?"

"I'm not a detective," I said. "I'm just a friend. I solved a murder once before and Phillip's son thinks I can solve this one, too."

He hooted with laughter. "Come in the back," he said then, with another up-and-down look.

Just then, a man walked in, and Adrian yelled toward the back of the store, "Hey, Fred, get out here. You got a customer." Adrian winked at me, opened a door at the end of the counter to let me through, and led me to the back room, which was full of boxes and metal junk. The back door was wide open, and a young kid, about eighteen, was unloading boxes from a truck and placing them in an empty corner.

"This is an auto parts business?" I said.

"Sure is," Adrian said.

"The name of it sounds more like a law firm."

"You like it? Gives the place a little class, don't it?"

I smiled with the left side of my mouth. "Who're the other Adrians?"

"Just me and Anton, my brother." He grinned and moved the toothpick up and down. "Get it? Adrian, Adrian—that's me—and Adrian—that's Anton. Adrian, Adrian and Adrian."

I pressed my lips together to ward off a smirk.

"Have a seat," he said, and he rolled a swivel desk chair toward me. I had to step aside to avoid being hit. That made him smile.

He sat down on another chair, leaned back and

splayed his legs, and gave me the toothpick leer again. "So," he said. "What sort of *help* did you have in mind?" He made the word "help" sound like an obscenity.

"I understand you were a client of Phillip Barry?" I said, wondering why in the world someone like Adrian would hire Phillip Barry as his accountant. Or why someone like Phillip Barry would even want Adrian as a client.

"My brother hired him," Adrian said, with a look of disgust.

"So, you own this business together?" I asked. I was trying to sound like I was just making pleasant conversation.

"Yeah," he said, not sounding the least bit pleased.

"Looks like he makes you do all the work, though, huh?"

Now that brightened his day. "You sure got that right," he said. Adrian draped his arm across the back of his chair, chewed his toothpick, and looked around the room. "Yeah, Anton shows his fat face around her every month or so just to remind everybody he owns the joint and then he splits. He never done one lousy thing from the time we set up shop."

"I thought you both owned it?" I said.

Adrian shrugged. "He put up the capital, I do the work."

"Oh, well, that's fair then, isn't it?"

Adrian's jaw tightened and he narrowed his eyes. "Well, I've heard of arrangements like that before," I said. "You didn't have to come up with any money and he doesn't have to spend any of his time."

Adrian looked at the wall. "Yeah. Well."

"What does he do for a living?"

"He's an attorney," Adrian said. "Anton Adrian, *Esquire*," he added with a derisive smile.

"Oh," I said, trying very hard not to show my surprise. "Does he have his own firm?"

"Him and some other guy. They do divorces and wills." Adrian leaned toward me and I could smell the smoke on his breath. "Get this," he said. "My hotshot attorney brother wrote up a will that left some old bag's money to her *dog*. Every penny, to a *dog*." He leaned back again, nodded his head, and smiled a crooked smile. "And he says I'm the one who's wasting my life."

I took a deep breath and forced a smile. "Do you have any idea why someone would want to kill Phillip Barry?"

Adrian gave me a sharp glance. "What makes you think I'd know?"

I shrugged. "No reason," I said. "I'm just trying to talk to everyone he knew and see if anyone has any ideas."

Adrian was trying to look casual but he was no longer chewing his toothpick.

"For instance," I said, "did he seem like the type of guy who would make enemies, or was he easy to get along with?"

"He was a decent enough dude," Adrian said.

"So you got along with him pretty well?"

"Sure," he said.

"So, I'll bet you were pretty upset when he wrote you that letter, huh?"

Adrian glowered at me. "What letter?" he snapped.

"The one he wrote to you very shortly before he was killed, about your receiving stolen property, embezzlement, and tax evasion." I raised my eyebrows at him and waited for a response.

"What business is that of yours?" he said.

"It may not be my business, but I'm sure the police will feel it's theirs. It sounds like a pretty good motive for murder, don't you think?"

"What does?" he said, giving me a look of utter disdain.

"Covering up all your illegal activities. It seems to me you had a pretty good reason to want to keep Phillip quiet."

"Lady, you're way off in left field. Man, you ain't even on the field. The cops knew all about that before Barry was even murdered." Adrian spit on the floor.

I frowned. "How did they know?"

"My brother turned me in," he growled, and spit on the floor again. I moved my chair back just a bit.

"Oh," I said with a dejected look.

"Oh, hey, sorry to disappoint you," he said. "You got some nerve, lady."

I sighed. "Did the police talk to you about Phillip's death?"

"Yeah, they talked to me," Adrian said. "Couple of days after he died. And I have an airtight alibi besides not having any motive. Guess they're a little more on the ball than you, huh?'' he added with a satisfied smirk.

Well, I guess they were. Darn that Brian.

As soon as I got home, I called him.

''Why didn't you tell me you already knew about Adrian Adrian?'' I said.

''Why didn't I tell *you?*'' Brian said.

''Yeah,'' I said. ''Why didn't you tell me? I wasted all my time, and...'' I stopped.

Brian didn't say anything.

''So, what was his alibi?'' I said.

''He was at a picnic for twelve hours with at least a hundred witnesses. Does that meet with your satisfaction?''

''Yes,'' I said, and abruptly changed the subject. ''When can Margaret Thurman pack up Anna's things?''

''She could do it now if she wants. Why?''

''I promised her I'd help her do the packing so I just wanted to know how long we'd have to wait.''

A few moments of silence. ''Nice of you,'' Brian said.

''Oh, give me a break, Brian. I'm just trying to help her out. There's a lot of stuff there and she doesn't have anyone else to help her.''

''Not to mention it gives you another opportunity to snoop around, doesn't it?''

I sighed. ''I assume,'' I said slowly, ''that you have already removed any pertinent evidence that was there. You *do* do that sort of thing, don't you?''

"Uh-huh."

"Did you find anything?"

Brian laughed but there was nothing good-natured about it. "We may have," he said, "but we're not in the habit of sharing the moment-by-moment results of official investigations with anyone who asks."

"Really," I said. "Well, I'm glad to hear it, Brian. I guess I just didn't realize that I was just *anyone.*"

He laughed again, this time with a little more friendliness. "You're not *just anyone,*" he said. "But I can't have you solving the case before me, can I? Wouldn't that make me look just a tad incompetent?"

"That's ridiculous," I said. "So what if someone figures something out before you did? It doesn't make you incompetent, it just makes you...slower."

No laugh that time. "I'll tell you what," he said. "Let's just see who's slower than whom. I'll bet you dinner at Fox & Hounds—champagne, the works— that I break this case before you do."

"You're crazy," I said.

"You know you can't do it. Admit it."

I closed my eyes and clenched my teeth. "Fine," I said. "If that's what you want, you're on."

I hung up, banged around the kitchen for about half an hour, and tried NordicTracking when I still hadn't calmed down. That worked pretty well, so I went up to bed and put That Homicide Detective out of my mind by thinking about Tom Hanson instead.

THE NEXT MORNING, at ten o'clock, Peter called.

"Did you find out who killed my dad yet?" he said

in a shaky voice.

"No, Peter, I'm sorry," I said. "But I do have some ideas, so I'm getting somewhere. And the police are working very hard, too, so don't worry, we'll figure it out."

"What ideas do you have?" His voice was full of tension and anxiety.

"Nothing definite," I said. "If I told you all of my suspicions, which include just about everybody, I might give you the wrong idea about someone. You don't want me to do that, do you?"

He sighed. "No, I guess not," he said.

"How are you doing?" I asked. "Do you want to come over?"

He hesitated. "No, that's okay," he said. "Thanks anyway. I'm okay, really."

"If you ever do want to come over, or just talk, no matter what time it is, I'll be here, okay?"

"Okay," he said softly. "I'll talk to you later." And he hung up.

I stared out the kitchen window for a bit and tried to tell myself not to feel guilty for not having solved the case yet, but it didn't work. I really had to get moving. It was killing Peter to wait and wait and it wasn't doing much for my good health, either. I had to *think*.

I went back into the library, told Janice and Emily I'd be in the kitchen for a while, and took my Phillip file with me. I read through all my notes, very carefully and slowly, and made a list of anyone and anything I hadn't covered. I'd talked to everyone in Phillip's family, some more than once, and everyone in Phillip's firm. I had no idea what to do next, and I was too depressed and angry with Brian to concentrate. I made myself a cup of tea, and when that didn't help, I decided to call Audrey. If she was in the mood, it would be the perfect time to take her up on her horseback-riding offer. As a matter of fact, it turned out to be an excellent idea, for more reasons than one.

SIXTEEN

"THAT WOULD BE WONDERFUL," Audrey said when I called her. "Would one-thirty be all right for you?"

"Perfect," I said, "Thanks, Audrey."

I felt better already. I worked a little more, ate lunch with Janice and Em, and changed into jeans and a sweatshirt.

"See you later," I said. "I'm going horseback riding."

They both looked somewhat surprised, to put it mildly. We took Audrey's car, at her suggestion, and drove North on US-43, toward Grafton. It was my first drive in a BMW. Not bad. Very comfortable. The day was absolutely beautiful. Bright blue skies with just a smattering of wispy clouds, a light breeze, almost no humidity, and temperatures in the mid-seventies. I knew Audrey was a kindred spirit when she left the windows open instead of using the air conditioner.

It took about forty minutes to reach the Grafton exit, another ten to get through Grafton, and then we drove down Highway 60 to Jackson.

"I wouldn't have to board so far away," Audrey told me with a look of apology, "but I had a high school chum who boarded her horses out here and I've always loved the area."

"It really is beautiful," I said. "It's so peaceful." Except for the tiny town of Grafton, and downtown Jackson, which you could miss in a blink, everything was farmland and marshes. Just miles and miles of grass and friendly cows. Somewhere between Jackson and West Bend, Audrey turned down a dirt road that brought us so far into the surrounding land that the main roads were no longer visible. Nothing but sun and wildflowers, unmown grass and paint-stripped buildings, rusted farm implements and a shiny green tractor. The buzz of an insect, a moo and a whinny, the cluck of a hen.

We walked through a field toward a distant building, and I heard some banging and some more whinnying, but still no human voices. Then we rounded a corner into a stable full of horses. One of the horses, a light tan one with white socks, was out of its stall, patiently succumbing to the brushing it was getting from a man wearing cutoff blue jeans, a faded red T-shirt, and a Brewers baseball cap. He was deeply tanned, and every facial expression he'd ever made was permanently etched in his face. When he saw us, he smiled and nodded.

"Afternoon, Mrs. Taylor," he said to Audrey.

"Hi, Bob," Audrey said. "This is Beth Hartley. Do you have someone nice and gentle for her? It's *almost* her first time. First time in many years, anyway."

Bob stopped his brushing and grinned at me. "I have just what you need," he said. He walked the tan-and-white horse toward a stall, and Audrey motioned me outside.

"He'll bring them around back," she said.

A few minutes later, Bob led a horse (one of those dark brown, medium-sized kind) from the barn, and handed the reins to Audrey. Audrey patted the horse and fed him some carrot pieces she had in her pocket. "This is Chocolate," she said with a wide grin. "Go ahead and pet him. He won't hurt you."

I moved, very hesitantly, toward the horse, and touched him gently. He made one of those snorting horse noises and whisked his tail back and forth. Audrey laughed when I jumped. "It's better to give them a firm pat," she said. "A light touch will only tickle him."

"Oh," I said, and wished I'd never suggested this.

"You'll be fine," Audrey said, as if she'd read my mind.

Then Bob brought me my horse, a smaller one with brown and white spots. He helped me on with a great show of patience, waited until I was ready, and went back in the barn. The horse (her name was Fairy) was really nice to me. Very gentle and calm, just like Bob had promised. Audrey gave me a few preliminary pointers, and we were off!

I was *terrified*—sure I'd fall off the horse, sure she'd run me into a tree, sure I was going to die. But pretty soon, I started to calm down. We rode through the open fields first, and then tried a path through the woods after I was more confident. The longer we rode, the more I liked it. And I actually liked it the *best* when we went fast.

"I *love* this," I said to Audrey, when we stopped for a rest.

Audrey smiled happily. "I do, too," she said. "I'm glad you enjoy it. You're welcome to come with me anytime. It's nice to have company."

I smiled. "I'd love to come again," I said.

We had stopped in a clearing near a small pond. Audrey helped me down and tied the horses to a nearby tree where they could still reach the water. The horses had a drink and Audrey and I sat down under another tree.

We talked about this and that, and after she'd asked about the investigation, she was quiet for a minute. "I have a confession to make," she said then.

I frowned and looked at her. "What do you mean?" I said.

"Well, it's not a confession, really, but I do have something to tell you that I didn't mention the first time we talked and I feel I should have."

I waited for her to go on.

Audrey took a deep breath and let it out. "I think Olivia and Gerry are having an affair."

I opened my eyes wide. "You're kidding?" I said. "What makes you think that?"

Audrey took another deep breath. "It was little things, at first. He kept looking at her across the table the last time we had them all to dinner. And she'd avert her eyes when she caught me watching them. Then I came into the kitchen and they were there together, alone, and they stopped talking when I came into the room. I know it doesn't sound like much, but it got me thinking. And then I saw them out together, in a restaurant, one day. I was with some of the women from my swim club, and there they were, having a quiet lunch in a dark corner.''

"Did they see you?" I said.

"I'm sure they didn't," Audrey said. "We were immediately shown to another dining room and they were too involved in their own conversation to notice."

"Are you absolutely positive, from the way they were acting, that they were having an affair, or do you think it's possible that you just interpreted it that way because you were already suspicious?"

Audrey sighed and thought for a while. "I suppose you're right, it could have been that. I guess I didn't really see anything that *couldn't* be interpreted innocently."

I nodded.

"But it certainly looked funny to me," she said.

"Well, I appreciate your telling me," I said. "And don't worry. No one will ever know I heard it from you."

"Thanks," Audrey said with a smile of relief.

I THOUGHT ABOUT the possibility of Olivia and Gerry, all the way home. My first thought was why would Olivia be interested? It seemed to me that Gerry would have less appeal to someone like Olivia than his brother had, in so many ways. They looked quite a bit alike, but Gerry was so much rougher, less classy, somehow. And he lacked Phillip's self-confident air. Then again, maybe all those things were what attracted her. Just the fact that he *was* different may have been enough.

It was a lot easier to understand Gerry's attraction to Olivia. She was not only beautiful and elegant, but very, very rich. Sue, who I found to be wonderful and far more attractive by my standards, may have seemed drab and unexciting in comparison.

"Guess what," I said to Janice and Emily when I got home.

Emily gave me a solicitous stare and Janice said, "What?"

"Olivia and Gerry may behaving an affair."

"Is that all these people do?" Emily said.

"That's what it looks like," I said.

"Are you sure they are?" Janice asked.

"No," I said, "but the person who told me knows both of them pretty well and she's pretty convinced."

"Olivia has a lot of money, right?" Emily said.

"Right."

"And she's pretty good-looking?"

"True."

"What does Gerry's wife look like?"

I told her.

"Where do they live?"

I told her.

"They did it," she said, and pretended to go back to work.

"Who did what?" I said.

"Gerry and Olivia killed Phillip," she said.

"*Why* would they do it?"

Emily gave me one of her looks. "Because they both wanted a better deal," she said. "Gerry wants more money and glamor and Olivia wanted Phillip's money."

"But most of the money was Olivia's."

"The operative word here, is 'most.' She was greedy. She wanted more." I raised my eyebrows and Emily gave me a satisfied smile.

"Maybe only one of them did it," Janice said. "And the other one is protecting the one who did it."

Now Emily raised her eyebrows. "You could be right," I said. "Now, the problem is, how in the world would I go about proving it?"

Emily shrugged. "How'd the meeting go with that Adrian guy yesterday?"

I laughed. "You should've seen this guy. He was all greasy and grimy and he kept giving me looks like he was going to jump on me."

"Lovely," Emily said. "You do meet the nicest men on a murder investigation."

I gave her a tight-lipped smile. "He has a brother who's an attorney," I said. "Anton Adrian. Have you ever heard of him?"

Emily wrinkled her brow and stared at me for quite some time. "Yeah," she said. "I think I have. His name is really familiar."

"He's a divorce lawyer, estates and trusts."

Emily frowned again and shook her head. "I don't know, but it'll come to me."

"Want to pay him a little visit and pretend you need a divorce?"

Janice gasped and stared at me with her mouth open. Emily laughed. "This is your hobby, not mine," she said. "If anyone's going to play divorce client, it's going to be you."

"Just thought I'd ask," I said, and gave Janice a wink. Janice smiled a little uncertainly, and went back to work.

IT WAS FRIDAY, AUGUST 1. At nine o'clock sharp, I received a call from Sharon Falk, and an invitation to visit her in her office.

"I believe I may have found what you're looking for," she said. "I'll be here all day, if you want to stop by."

"I'll be right there," I said.

When I arrived, Denise told me Sharon was waiting for me and I should go right in. Her door was open, and she was at her desk, reading. When I knocked lightly on the doorjamb, she looked up, directed me to a chair (now empty), and waited for me to sit down.

"If you don't mind," she said a bit tersely, "I'd like to get another little matter out of the way before we discuss the murder."

"Sure," I said with a shrug.

"I don't know quite how to put this," she said. "I'm curious about why you thought it necessary to mention my private and, incidentally, rather innocuous relationship with Phillip Barry to his brother."

I opened my eyes wide and gaped at her. "You mean *you* had an affair with Phillip, too?"

She stiffened and turned a dark red. "It wasn't you," she said, more as a statement than a question.

"No," I said as I shook my head. "When did you have an affair with him?"

She gave me an annoyed look, but it quickly disappeared. "It went on for about four years," she said in a resigned tone of voice, "but it ended last Christmas. It's ancient history. It didn't mean anything when it was going on and it doesn't mean anything now."

Well, that sounded like fun. "What happened?" I said. "Why'd you end it?"

"He ended it," she said. "It was the usual go-around. I couldn't understand why he couldn't spend a little time with me and Doodle on Christmas—just once—and he couldn't understand why I couldn't understand. So he decided he'd had enough and he ended it." Sharon laughed a little uncomfortably and looked across the room. "It was just as well," she said. "It wasn't going anywhere and it was never going to."

She looked back at me and shrugged, and I gave her a sympathetic smile. I really did feel bad for her. She seemed almost grateful to have someone to talk to, even if it was someone she didn't particularly care for.

"I'm sorry," I said.

She attempted a smile and shrugged again.

"Did you say you and *Doodle?*" I asked.

Sharon took a framed picture from her desk drawer and held it up for me to see. "My daughter," she said with a smile. "Her real name was Amanda but we called her Yankee Doodle because she was born on the Fourth of July. Then it got shortened to Doodle."

I smiled and she put the picture away. "She sure is cute," I said.

Sharon nodded.

"Do you have any other children?"

She shook her head. Then she handed me a piece of paper. "There's your murderer," she said with a look of pride.

I turned it over. It was the same letter from Phillip to Adrian Adrian. I opened my mouth to say something, and closed it again. I read it slowly, and made occasional comments as I did, such as "Oh, my gosh" and "I can't believe this." Then I looked at Sharon with a big grin.

"This is great," I said. "Where did you find this?"

"In the client's file. It was one of the ones I had to go through but I didn't get to it until this morning."

I had another moment when I considered telling her that both I and the police already knew about Adrian (and that he was almost surely innocent) but she seemed so pleased with herself and I didn't want to spoil it for her.

"I'll let you know what happens," I said instead. "Maybe I'll pay this guy a visit."

She raised her eyebrows. "Isn't that a bit risky?" she said. "Especially after what happened to Anna?"

I gave her a brave smile. "I'll be careful," I said.

BEFORE I LEFT the building, I stopped in to see Gerry.

"Beth," Gerry said. "Sit down."

His hair was neatly combed, his tie was on straight, but his eyelids looked weighted and his face was pale.

I gave him a weak smile. "How're you doing?" I asked.

He shook his head in response.

"I had dinner with Tom Hanson the other day."

He nodded slightly.

"He thinks Olivia knew about Phillip's affairs, too," I said.

A bored shrug.

"Do you think Phillip knew about *Olivia's* affairs?"

Gerry abruptly lifted his head and stared at me.

"Do you think he knew about *you* and Olivia?"

Gerry opened his mouth as if to answer, then blew out his breath. "How did you know?" he said.

"It doesn't matter," I said. "I can't tell you how I know."

He gave me a helpless look.

"I'm sorry," I said. "I didn't mean to upset you. I don't know why I blurted it out like I did. I hadn't really intended to."

He waved his hand at me and shook his head. Then he let out a big sigh and stared at the wall. "It started last year," he said quietly. "Olivia guessed about Phillip and Sharon and she came to me about it. It really got to her. More than the others, I mean. She was afraid he was going to leave her."

I frowned. "Why would she worry more about Sharon than anyone else?"

"I don't know," Gerry said. "She said she sensed that it was serious. I don't know," he added with a wave of his hand. "It didn't make any sense, but I did my best to calm her down."

Yeah, you sure did. "So that's how things got started between you and Olivia?"

Gerry nodded. "Neither of us had intended for it to happen, but we saw a lot of each other and it was just that sort of situation. She started to depend on me and it felt good to be needed again. I don't expect you to understand."

"No, I do. I can understand how that could happen. I'm sorry to get into all this personal stuff with you, but it's important to know all these things if I'm going to have any chance of coming up with the answer."

Gerry nodded. "Don't worry about it," he said. "It almost feels good to get it off my chest."

I smiled. "Did you ever talk to Phillip about Olivia knowing about Sharon?"

"Yeah. Believe it or not, he was more upset about Olivia coming to me than he was about her knowing about the affair."

"Do you know if he ever talked to Sharon about it?"

Gerry raised his brows. "Well, he must have, because it was shortly after that that he broke it off with her."

"Did Olivia know that?" I said.

"Yeah, I told her," Gerry said. "I waited a few

weeks before I did, though. I wasn't sure if he meant to go through with it and I was also afraid it would change things between me and Olivia."

"Did it?" I asked.

Gerry gave me a little smile. "No, it didn't," he said.

I sighed. I had to fight feeling glad for him, so I forced myself to think about Sue.

"Does Sue know?" I said.

Gerry's face turned red. "I don't think so," he said. "You have to understand—" He broke off. "Never mind," he said. "I'm just making excuses."

"It's okay," I said. I thought for a few moments. "Do you think it's possible that Phillip had promised something permanent to Sharon and that he changed his mind only because of Olivia's reaction?"

Gerry frowned and shook his head. "I imagine it's possible," he said, "but I'd be awfully surprised if he had. As far as I knew, he'd never intended to leave Olivia."

"Why? Did he believe he loved her, or what?"

"I don't know," Gerry said. "But he did lead a very comfortable life, owing in no small part to Olivia and her money."

"Do you think Sharon Falk could have killed him because he left her?"

"No," Gerry said. "He left her…what? Seven months before he was killed? If she was going to kill him because he dumped her, she would've done it then, not now, seven months later."

"Yeah, I guess you're right," I said.

"Have you gotten any closer to solving this thing than you were the last time I talked to you?" Now he was sounding impatient and a little annoyed.

I took a deep breath. "No," I said in a steady voice. "It isn't the easiest thing in the world to solve something like this, you know, and I do have a business to run. I haven't been able to devote my every waking moment to this investigation."

He started to say something but I stopped him.

"The police are investigating this too, and they haven't solved it yet, either," I added.

Gerry massaged his forehead, then ran his hand through his hair. He sat back in his chair and looked at me.

"I'm sorry," he said. "This whole thing is really starting to get to me. I just want it behind me so I can get on with my life. I suppose you think that's pretty selfish."

"No," I said. "I don't. You just want to get it settled in your mind so you can start to deal with it. It doesn't mean you don't care. You just need to know what happened before you can start learning to live with it."

Gerry awarded me a smile. It was pretty weak, but I could tell he meant it.

WHEN I GOT HOME, Mrs. Gunther was in the kitchen having a cup of tea. I made myself a cup and joined her. She studied me for a few moments and frowned. "What's the matter?" she said.

"Oh, nothing," I said with a sigh. "I'm just frustrated, I guess."

"It's not just this case that's bothering you," she said. "You can't hide anything from me, honey. I see everything that goes on in this house. Now tell me what's really bothering you."

I stared at her and then I grinned. "You're right," I said. "You *do* see everything that goes on in this house. Why didn't I think of that before?"

She gave me a very peculiar look as I picked up the phone.

SEVENTEEN

"OLIVIA?" I SAID. "This is Beth. I was wondering if you'd mind if I talked to your housekeeper."

A slight pause. "Are you experiencing domestic difficulties, Beth?"

"No," I said with an admirable amount of self-control. "I'd like to talk with her about Phillip to see if she might know something."

"I take this to mean you've been unsuccessful in your investigation?"

"Well, I haven't solved the murder yet, if that's what you mean. But the more people I talk to, the more likely I'll be able to do that, sometime in the future."

"I see," she said in a patronizing voice.

"Would it be possible for me to see her today?"

"Really, Beth," she said. "This is getting a little out of hand, don't you think?"

I didn't answer.

"Very well," she said, to fill the silence. "Come over now, if you must."

"I'll be right there," I said. "Thanks, Olivia."

Olivia opened the door herself, wearing a white linen skirt and matching sleeveless blouse. Beige sandals, gold jewelry. Same hairdo.

"Thank you for being so punctual," she said.

I tried my best to smile.

She led me to the room at the front of the house that looks like it's never used except to keep guests waiting. When she opened the doors (pocket doors, like the ones in my library), I saw her housekeeper, Marie, sitting on the edge of one of the silk-covered sofas (light mauve), her hands in her lap, fidgeting with her apron.

"Marie," Olivia said, and the woman jumped. "Please answer Miss Hartley's questions to the best of your ability."

Marie nodded at Olivia and then at me. She continued the fidgeting and her brow was creased. Olivia turned and walked out, and closed the doors behind her.

I smiled at Marie. "Did Mrs. Barry tell you why I'm here?" I asked her.

"About Mr. Barry," she said with a squeak.

"Did the police talk to you after Mr. Barry was murdered?"

She nodded, still fidgeting.

"You don't have to be nervous about this," I said. "You're not going to get in any trouble. Mrs. Barry *wants* you to talk to me."

Fidget, fidget.

"How long have you worked for Mrs. Barry?" I asked her, thinking I could ease my way into it.

"Ten years," Marie said. "Ten years, two months, and three days."

"That's a long time," I said, trying not to laugh. "My housekeeper, Mrs. Gunther, has worked for me for only six years, but she worked for my Aunt Sarah for *twenty-five* years before that.''

''Oh, my goodness,'' Marie said, her eyes bugging out. ''Imagine that.''

''She only works on Mondays, Wednesdays, and Fridays, though. Do you work for Mrs. Barry everyday?''

Marie nodded. ''Monday through Friday,'' she said. ''Sometimes weekends, if there's a special to-do.''

''Did you know Mr. Barry very well?''

Her look was wary now, and a little nervous, but nothing like before. ''Not very, no,'' she said.

''Did you ever hear him arguing with anyone? Did anyone ever give him any trouble while you were around?''

She started fidgeting again.

''Didn't the police ask you these questions?'' I said.

She harrumphed. ''I don't tell them anything,'' she said.

''Well, if you tell *me*,'' I said, ''I promise I won't go running straight to the police with anything you say.''

She gave me a skeptical look.

''Please,'' I said. ''Actually, I'm having a sort of *race* with the police to see who can solve the murder first.''

She opened her mouth and stared at me.

''So I won't tell them anything you tell me,'' I said,

"unless of course you know for sure who did it. I guess then I'd have to tell."

She frowned and looked at me askance. "Is that right?" she said.

"I'm not kidding," I said. "I know the detective who's working on the case. Well, actually, I'm sort of dating him, and he said there was no way I could solve it before he did and he dared me to do it so we're having a race."

"Well, I'll be a…" She gave me a nod. "You just ask me anything," she said. "Anything you want to know."

"Okay," I said. "Tell me if you ever heard any arguing."

"Oh, I hear all kinds of arguing," Marie said. "Arguing all the time."

"Really?" I said.

"Oh, yes," she said with a wrinkled brow. "Mr. Barry argued with everybody."

"Like whom, for instance?"

"He argued with Mrs. Barry and Mr. Paul all the time. They were always going at each other. It was enough to drive me nuts. And he had a *big* fight with Mr. Gerry right before he died."

"How soon before he died?"

She gave me a pointed look and lowered her voice. "Couldn't have been more than two, three days before."

"Could you hear what they were saying?"

Marie looked at the door, leaned toward me, and

whispered, "They were fighting over Mrs. Barry, and both of them were plenty mad."

I raised my eyebrows and tried to look shocked. "What did they say, exactly? Can you remember?"

She looked at the door again, and back at me. "Mr. Barry told Mr. Gerry to stay away from Mrs. Barry."

"Was Mrs. Barry home at the time?"

Marie shook her head. "It was her weekly bridge game."

"So they knew she'd be gone?"

Marie nodded.

"Was this at night or during the day?"

"Evening, 'round seven. Every Tuesday she has her bridge game."

"Why were you here so late?"

"Mrs. Barry asked me to stay special and do the silver on account of she was having guests the next day."

"Did Mr. Barry know you were in the house?"

"No, he didn't," she said.

"Did you hear anything else?"

"Nothing more than what I told you. He just told him to keep away from what was his."

"What did Gerry say?"

Marie's expression changed from a smirk to a scowl. "He said there was no way he was going to stay away from her as long as she wanted him. They were all adults, he said, and they could choose their own lives."

"Can you remember any of the arguments you heard between Mr. Barry and Paul, or Mrs. Barry?"

Marie gave the door a furtive glance and lowered her voice again. "I heard him ask Mrs. Barry where the 'H' she was, plenty of times."

"Did he ever mention Gerry's name to her?"

"Not that I heard, no, he didn't."

"What about Paul? Could you hear any of what they said?"

Marie adopted a look of disapproval. "Yes, I did," she said. "But I wish I hadn't. Mr. Paul has a mouth on him, I won't deny it, but even so, it was no way to treat the boy."

"What did he say to him?"

"It was always the same thing. Work, work, work. If you want my opinion, Mr. Paul never wanted to be an accountant like Mr. Barry, but he never gave the poor boy a choice, far as I could tell. I heard him one day, just last month, telling Mr. Paul to clean up his act and get ready for his exam. Said he wanted him behind a desk and hard at work the day after graduation. Just imagine. No vacation, no time for celebrating or nothing."

I raised an eyebrow and sighed. "Do *you* have any ideas about who killed Mr. Barry?" I said.

Marie looked at the door again, leaned as close to me as she could without falling off her seat, and whispered, "My bets are on Mr. Gerry and the Mrs."

"You really think so?" I said.

"That's my bet," Marie said. "My sister-in-law, she thinks Mr. Paul did it." My eyes widened. "Paul?" I said. "Why?"

"Money," she whispered. "From what I hear, he

comes into a truckload on account of Mr. Barry's passing."

"Does your sister-in-law know the family?" I asked.

"Only from what I tell her," she said, "and I tell her plenty."

"Well," I said, standing to leave, "if you think of anything else, would you let me know?"

"I sure will," Maric said. "I sure will." I gave her my card.

EMILY, JANICE, AND Mrs. Gunther were already gone when I got home, so I added some notes to my Phillip file and made myself a dinner of penne with grated cheese and a salad. I took it out to the screened porch with my mystery, and stayed out there until seven o'clock, when the phone rang.

It was Margaret Furman. She was coming the next morning to pack up Anna's things. I agreed to pick her up at the airport at ten-fifteen and drive her straight to the apartment. If we worked at it, we could have everything done by early afternoon.

SATURDAY, AUGUST 2. I got up at eight, showered and dressed, ate a leisurely breakfast of English muffins and tea, and left for the airport. Margaret's plane was on time and she had no luggage, so we were out of there in less than ten minutes. She was quiet on the way over, and every attempt I made to start a conversation was met with one-worded responses. I decided to let her alone since she was clearly in no mood to socialize.

Margaret had arranged, the night before, for Mr. Royce to leave the keys under the mat in case he was gone when we arrived. When we let ourselves in, I turned to Margaret, and she had tears in her eyes. I pretended not to notice and kept quiet until she seemed to be all right.

"What do you plan to do with the furniture?" I asked her then.

"I have arranged for someone to pick it up next week. It will be sold."

I nodded. That was a good idea. "Where'd all these boxes come from?" I said.

"I asked the company who will move Anna's furniture to leave me some for packing," she said. "They will deliver them, too."

"Well, where would you like to start?" I said, marveling at her efficiency.

Margaret took a deep breath and let it out. Her lip quivered and I was afraid she was going to cry, but she didn't.

"I think I will start with the bedroom," she said in an unsteady voice. "Perhaps you could empty the desk?"

"Sure," I said. "Just put everything in a box?"

She nodded.

I waited until she was out of the room and got to work. I was able to fit everything into one box rather easily, and I took my time in case I'd spot something

I'd missed before—but I didn't. I closed the box and labeled it "Desk."

I was about to start on the closets but I decided to check on Margaret first. It was awfully quiet in there. In fact, I hadn't heard a sound since she'd left me.

When I opened the door, I saw her, perfectly still, sitting on the edge of the bed staring straight in front of her.

"Are you all right?" I said gently.

She raised her head, very slowly, lines creasing her brow. She glanced in my direction, but it was an unfocused look. After several moments, when she still hadn't responded, I walked over and sat on the bed. She started to tremble and covered her face with her hands. When I put my arm around her, she started to cry.

"I can't do this," she said a little later. "All of Anna's things. So many..." Her voice faded away.

"Would you like me to do it for you?" I said. "You can even stay at my house while I finish the packing if it's too difficult for you to be here."

She looked at me with tears running down her cheeks. "You are so kind," she said. "How can I ever thank you?"

I smiled sadly. "You already have," I said.

I drove Margaret to my house, made her a cup of tea and some toast, and told her I'd be back as soon as I could.

I went back to the apartment, let myself in again, and started right in on the closets. Anna had so little in the way of clutter that it was a relatively easy job.

I put the clothes and linens in separate boxes and used another one for the framed photographs, wall pictures, and the snapshots in Anna's hatbox. I looked through those again, even more carefully than the first time, but nothing new appeared. I went to the bedroom then, and added the clothes from her drawers and closet to the others I'd left in the living room. I checked all the pockets, and every nook and cranny, but found nothing the least bit enlightening. The weight room, I left for the movers, with the exception of the posters and Phillip's dart-embellished picture. Why was Anna so angry with Phillip? I would've loved to know the answer to that one.

I saved the kitchen for last, which took the longest, since I had to wrap the glassware and dishes, but I was done with everything by a quarter to two. I locked up, went downstairs, and knocked on Mr. Royce's door.

"Well, if it isn't you again," he said in a friendly voice when he opened the door. "What can I do for you, Miss?"

I explained my presence and returned the keys. "I was also hoping I could talk to you for a few minutes about Anna," I said then, and gave him a plaintive look.

"Sure you can," he said. "Come right on in." He held the door open for me and I walked under his arm.

The entrance to his flat was directly into the living room, with no foyer. The room was square, painted a light green, with brown, green, and gold wall-to-wall carpeting with a little swirly design. There was a couch against the wall opposite the door, covered completely by an old bedspread. A grease spot shone on the wall above the couch, near the end table. The table was painted the same color as the wall. It held an ashtray with two cigar stubs, a glass full of something amber-colored, and a *TV Guide*. Newspapers were piled on the floor between the table legs.

He had a light blue vinyl recliner in front of the TV, a gold armchair, and two more tables, one pine and the other oak. There was a picture on one wall of a sea captain peering out over a velvet sea.

"Have yourself a seat," Mr. Royce said, and he gestured at the couch.

I sat on the very edge and tried to look comfortable. He sat in the gold chair, which faced the couch. Then he started to get up again.

"May I offer you some refreshment?" he asked.

"No. No, thank you," I said. "I'll just be a minute. I really have to get going. Anna's sister is waiting for me at my house and I told her I'd be back as soon as I could. I just wanted to ask you if you'd ever heard or seen anything suspicious while Anna was living here."

Mr. Royce frowned and ran his hand over his head. "Well, now, I can't say as I recall anything of that nature. Can't say as I ever heard much from her at all. Not even from her little dog."

I smiled. "I just thought, maybe by chance, you might have heard or seen something that would give us a clue as to who killed her."

He put on a pensive face, and shook his head. "Nope," he said with decisiveness. "Never heard or saw a thing. Never even had a visitor, far as I knew. 'Cept for her sister, that is." He nodded. "Mighty fine woman, her sister. Margaret, isn't it?"

I smiled. "Yes, that's right," I said. "Well, thanks for your time, Mr. Royce. I'd better get back to her."

"Give her my regards, won't you?" he said. "And tell her I'm mighty sorry about Anna. Mighty sorry."

"I will, Mr. Royce. Thanks."

WHEN I GOT BACK HOME, Margaret was staring out my kitchen window. She turned and smiled at me when I walked in. She looked a hundred percent better than she had when I'd left her. We had another cup of tea, talked for a little while, and then I drove her to the airport and said good-bye, promising to keep her informed.

That night, Janice and I went out for pizza at Balistreri's, in Wauwatosa. I wasn't in the mood for staying home alone, and neither was she.

"I kind of miss Scamper," she said after we'd ordered.

"Yeah, me too," I said.

She asked me how the investigation was going and we talked about nothing else through a large pizza with almost everything but anchovies, and a couple glasses of wine.

"I don't know," Janice said. "He sure must've made a lot of women unhappy. And also their *husbands*. I still think Olivia could've done it. She really has the best motive. All the other women could've been dumped by him, but it's got to be a lot worse to be rejected when it's your own husband.''

"Yeah, I know," I said. "But I just can't see her doing it."

"What about Gerry? Isn't the whole accounting business his, now?"

"Yeah, but he has to buy Phillip's shares. It's not like he gets it for nothing. Besides that, Phillip was his own brother. I really can't see him doing it."

"What about Paul?"

"His own son?" I said.

"You know, I read somewhere that most people are murdered by people they know and the family members are always the first they suspect, not the last."

"Well, that's true," I said. "I guess I should stop thinking that way. I just have such a hard time understanding how someone could kill their own father or brother. Husbands I can understand a little better, but even that seems weird to me. Why don't people just get divorced?"

"Beats me," Janice said.

"Maybe I should talk to Paul again. I know a lot more about him now than I did the first time, and maybe he wouldn't be so closed up now."

"Couldn't hurt to try," Janice said.

I went to bed early that night, wondering how much trouble Olivia would give me the next morning when I asked to talk to Paul again.

EIGHTEEN

"YOU'VE TAKEN ENOUGH of his time," was what she said. "I see no reason why you need to talk with him again."

"So you're refusing to let me talk to him?" I asked, knowing how people hate to be accused of such things.

"I…certainly I'm not *refusing* to let you see him," she said.

"So you will let me talk to him?"

A rather lengthy hesitation and a loud sigh. "Just a moment," she said in an angry voice. "I'll get him."

"Paul speaking," he said when he picked up the phone.

"Paul, this is Beth Hartley. I know this is a lot to ask, but I was wondering if I could talk to you one more time. I have something to tell you that I think you'll be interested in."

"Uh, sure," he said.

"Would you mind coming over here this time? I think we could talk more freely."

He hesitated, but then agreed. He said he'd be over in twenty minutes.

I ate a quick breakfast and had two cups of tea while I waited. He was here at nine-twenty, exactly.

He wore a light blue Izod shirt, navy cuffed shorts, and leather docksiders with no socks. Very preppy. I offered him coffee or tea, but he declined. He remained standing, though I offered him a seat, and he looked as if he might bolt any minute.

I decided to get right to the point before I lost him. "Did you know that your father wanted to go to law school when he was young and that he'd even been accepted to a few law schools but his father wouldn't let him go?"

Paul's face turned red, his expression a mixture of shock and pain. He sat down and stared at the floor.

"I didn't think you knew," I said softly. "But I thought you'd want to. Your Aunt Audrey told me about it."

He still wasn't looking at me, so I went on. "I know he gave you very little choice about your own career but I thought it might help you to understand why he did it if you knew he'd gone through the same thing himself. He was treating you the same way his father treated him."

Paul looked up then, and his expression was one of righteous indignation. "And you think that *excuses* him?" he said. "That makes it all the worse. He knew how I felt but he still treated me that way. He wanted to louse up my life just like my grandfather loused up his." He suddenly laughed, but it was bitter and full of desperation. "Do you know what *I've* always wanted to be? I want to be a lawyer. I've been accepted at three different law schools. My dad would've killed me if he knew."

"Maybe he would've understood perfectly," I said, "if you'd told him about it. Maybe he would have wanted you to go."

His laugh changed to a frightening giggle.

"Were you ever going to tell him?" I said.

He looked at me as if I'd just entered the world. "I hadn't made up my mind," he said, suddenly calm. "I didn't know what to do."

"What are you going to do now?"

"I don't know," he said. "I have no idea."

I didn't ask him anymore questions. I'd already learned what I wanted to know.

Paul went home and I spent the day reading and lolling around in the yard. I was more perplexed than ever about Phillip's death, and the next day's news didn't help one bit.

ON MONDAY MORNING, as Emily was pouring herself a cup of coffee, she said, "Remember I told you Anton Adrian's name sounded so familiar to me? It came to me last night. I'm pretty sure I read something about him being suspended for professional misconduct."

"Did it have anything to do with embezzlement or tax evasion?" I said.

She frowned. "It might've been for tax evasion."

"Where did you read it?"

"The *Journal*, I think."

"Do you remember when it was?"

She shook her head. "No, but it was sometime this year."

I sighed. "Well, I guess I'll just have to look through all the back issues."

"Sorry," she said. "I'll come with you if you want."

"Great," I said with a grin. "You want to go now?"

She grunted and grabbed her purse.

We drove to the library in Emily's car, I'm sorry to say, and drove around for twenty-five minutes until we found a parking space on the street. She refused to let me pay for a lot, and she certainly wasn't going to pay for it.

When we finally got inside, we had to wait in a long line just to request the microfilm, and then another to use one of the machines. So it was close to an hour later before I was looking through the back issues of the *Milwaukee Journal Sentinel* for the goods on Anton Adrian.

"There it is," Emily whispered hoarsely, about fifteen minutes after we'd started. "That's the article."

It was the March tenth edition of the paper. Not front-page news, but interesting, nevertheless:

On the fifth of this month, the Wisconsin Supreme Court suspended the law license of Anton Adrian, 37, of Milwaukee, for 90 days, for professional misconduct in the representation of a client.

The article went on to describe the misconduct in question, something involving the sale of a client's business assets to Adrian's wife without adequate disclosure. The court found that Adrian had engaged in conduct involving dishonesty, deceit, and misrepresentation in violation of SCR 20:8.4(c). Nothing about income tax evasion, though.

"I thought you said it had to do with tax evasion?" I whispered to Emily.

"Well, I wasn't sure," she whispered back. "You're the one who put that idea in my head."

We looked for another forty minutes, just to make sure there wasn't anything else, and then went home. When we got there, I looked through an entire year's worth of legal journals, but found nothing there, either, except for the matter detailed in the newspaper.

"Why're you so interested in finding out if he did anything else?" Emily said.

"I wanted to see if he'd been implicated in his brother's crimes. Although I'm not sure why I care," I added. "Something about it bothers me, but I don't know what. Well, the very least I know is that I shouldn't trust anything he might say to me."

Emily gave me a condescending smirk. "You ought to feel that way about anyone you talk to, particularly in this context," she said.

"Yeah, I guess you're right."

When we broke for lunch, I looked in the yellow pages for Anton Adrian's firm. It would've been hard to miss. He had an ad that took up almost a quarter of a page. Downtown Milwaukee location, too. Not bad. Next, I pulled out my Martindale and Hubbel (which contains a listing and résumé of most law-firm lawyers) and checked out his background. Marquette Law School, law review, moot court, cum laude graduate. This was greasy, grimy Adrian Adrian's brother?

At six o'clock, after everyone had gone home, I called Anton Adrian's office and asked to speak to him.

"What is this in regard to?" the receptionist said.

"My name is Beth Hartley," I said, "and this is in regard to the death of Phillip Barry."

He was on the line almost immediately. "Miss Hartley," he said in a refined sort of voice. "This is Anton Adrian. How can I help you?"

"Are you really the brother of Adrian Adrian?" I asked.

"Yes, I am," he said after a slight pause.

"And you are a client of the Phillip Barry firm?"

"What is this about, if I may ask?"

"I'm a close friend of the family," I said, "and I am helping to investigate Mr. Barry's murder at the request of his son. I was hoping you could help me."

"How might I do that?" His tone was polite and patient, but not particularly friendly.

"I'd like to talk to you about Phillip, if you can spare the time. I promise to keep it short. I'm talking to as many people as I can to see if anyone has any ideas or information that might lead me to his killer."

Anton sighed. "I see," he said. "I'm afraid I can't be of any assistance to you. I knew Mr. Barry only in a professional capacity. I met with him personally only three, maybe four times. Most of our business was conducted by telephone or through correspondence.''

My next question was sure to annoy him, but I was dying to know the answer so I took a chance. ''Why would you want to put up the capital for your brother's auto parts business?''

No answer.

''Mr. Adrian?''

''That is a personal business matter that could have no conceivable connection to the death of Phillip Barry,'' he said.

''What made you seek out Phillip Barry's services to begin with?''

''He came highly recommended,'' Anton said. ''Miss Hartley, if there's nothing more, I have a client waiting. Good day.''

''Thank you for your time,'' I said, but he'd already hung up.

I wasn't sure what to make of him. He didn't seem to like me much.

TUESDAY, AUGUST 5, the fateful day.

I worked until five, when Janice and Emily went home, had a light supper of fruit salad and tea, and worked some more. At seven, when I received another frantic call from Peter asking if I'd solved the case *yet*, I put my work away and brought out the Phillip file. I read and reread everything, and tried as hard as I could to come up with an answer, but I just couldn't do it. When I started to lose all hope that I'd ever figure it out, I knew I was in big trouble. I'd never accomplish anything if I lost all my confidence. I had to get out and clear my mind, and just *think*.

I left the file on the table, put on my walking shoes, went outside, and just started walking—from Newberry to Maryland, up Frederick, down Murray, then Bradford, Webster, and Belleview, and all the way to Locust. It was a cool night, barely seventy degrees. A gentle breeze rustled the trees and normal, everyday noises filled the air—the sound of dishes being removed from a cupboard, a television turned up a bit too high, music playing in an upstairs bedroom, muffled voices, the sputter of a sprinkler, the bark of a dog. I walked and walked until I forgot where I was, mulling everything over, running every little detail through my head. The names of everyone I'd talked to, everything I'd seen. Possible motives, opportunity, guilty behavior. And unexplained coincidences. Like Anna.

Anna had to be my best and strongest clue, I decided as I picked up my pace. She knew who the killer was. In fact, she knew the killer. And so did Phillip. *Both Phillip and his secretary knew the killer.*

Could the fact that Anna was Phillip's secretary be mere coincidence, or was it the reason for their mutual acquaintance with the killer? And who would they both know? Certainly anyone at the firm, possibly anyone connected with the business. The Adrian brothers or any of Phillip's clients. Joanne Donnelly, Eunice Waters, Denise Shaw. Bob Hennison and Louise Beaumont. Gerry or Sharon Falk. What about Phillip's family? Surely they'd all met his secretary.

I eliminated the Friedmans, Tom Hanson, and Sam Goldstein. And Miriam Beechman, Patricia Morgan, and Sandra Goldberg. And Audrey. And Marie. And Haley and Peter.

Who was left? Gerry. Now, *he* was a good possibility—free reign with Olivia, revenge for earlier wrongs, maybe a chance for long-term financial gain now that the business was all his? Olivia was another obvious candidate—neglected wife of a philandering husband, wealthy and greedy enough not to want to give up anything in a divorce. Paul? Resentful and angry—and the timing was good, shortly before his twenty-first birthday. The Adrians? No. Sharon Falk—jilted lover, but in her case the timing was wrong. Joanne Donnelly, Eunice Waters, and Denise Shaw? No known motive. I eliminated all three of them and did the same for Bob Hennison and Louise Beaumont (and the rest of Phillip's clients, since I knew nothing about them). That left Gerry, Olivia, Paul, and Sharon.

I was at least ten blocks from home by then and it had started to rain. For a few minutes it was no more than a drizzle, but then it really began to pour. I turned around and headed for home, walking faster and faster, running everything through my mind until it was nothing but a big blur. Timing, motive, gain, revenge. Timing, motive...timing.

Timing. No way...it *couldn't* be.

I looked at my watch. It was eight-ten. I had just about enough time to make it. I ran the rest of the way home, bolted upstairs, took off my clothes, dried myself off, and grabbed the first thing I could find. Then I went for my car and drove to the public library.

I parked in the lot, stood in line for what seemed like hours, and then ran through the two weeks' worth of newspapers I'd requested.

I found what I was looking for in the December twenty-sixth edition:

Amanda Falk. Born 7-4-87. Died 12-25-96. Survived by her mother, Sharon A. Falk, her father Joseph P. Falk, and her maternal grandmother, Dolores M. Bouchard.

I read it again. And again.

I returned the microfilm, retrieved my car, and drove home in a daze. It seemed like such a farfetched idea, but everything fit if I was right.

I had to talk to Gerry. It was late, after nine o'clock, but I called him anyway.

"He's still at the office," Sue said. "If it's really important, you can call him there."

"Thanks, Sue," I said. "I'll do that."

I dialed the office number, praying he wasn't out with Olivia rather than working like a good little husband.

He was there.

"Gerry," I said. "I have to talk to you. Now. I think I know who killed Phillip."

He hesitated a moment, and said, "Okay, but you'll

have to come here. I'm working on something that has to be finished by tomorrow morning."

"Fine," I said. "I'll be right there."

Ten minutes later, I'd arrived, even more sure of my theory than I'd been when I left. Gerry opened the door as soon as I rang the bell. He looked funny—sort of pale and shaky—but I didn't think too much of it at the time since I'd seen him look that way before. He didn't say anything to me, just sort of waved me in. When I got inside I was just about to say something to him when I jumped and sucked in my breath.

"Why didn't you tell me she was here?" I said in a squeaky voice.

"You didn't *ask* me," he hissed back.

Sharon directed us toward Gerry's office with a wave of her gun. We did as she asked, and neither of us looked back. Gerry was ahead of me and I could see his knees wobble. The back of his shirt was soaking wet.

When we got inside, Sharon closed the door and told us both to stand with our backs to the wall. She kept the gun aimed at us and moved back toward the desk. I watched her carefully, trying my best to remain calm, but I couldn't stop shaking.

She looked at me, then Gerry, and back at me. Her expression was more troubled than cocky, more sad than angry. She looked ready to cry.

"You should've stayed out of it," she said to me, in an almost tender, merely chiding manner. "It wasn't your concern. This was between me and Phillip, no one else.''

I gave her a look of pity, and understanding. ''You did it for your daughter, didn't you?'' I said gently. ''You killed him because of Amanda.''

Sharon nodded and her eyes filled with tears. ''He killed her,'' she cried. ''She wouldn't have died if it hadn't been for him.''

Gerry scrunched up his face and looked from Sharon to me. ''Her daughter?'' he said. He looked back at Sharon. ''Your *daughter?*'' He'd raised his voice to a high-pitched whine. ''She died in a car accident. Phillip wasn't even involved. *You were driving.*''

Sharon started to cry and the gun began to wobble.

''She was upset about Phillip,'' I said to Gerry. ''He'd just broken up with her and she was very upset. She was so upset she got into an accident and Amanda was killed. And she feels Phillip was responsible because he was the one who upset her so much.'' I looked to Sharon for confirmation. She nodded vigorously, tears streaming from her eyes, the gun pointed at the floor.

''But that was last Christmas,'' Gerry said with a frantic look. ''Why now?'' He was addressing me rather than Sharon.

I swallowed hard in an attempt to fight the lump I felt in my throat. ''Her birthday,'' I said in a quavering voice. ''She killed him on Amanda's birthday.''

Gerry's eyes opened wide and he gaped at Sharon. ''The Fourth of July,'' he whispered.

Sharon was sobbing so hard she was gulping air. Her entire body was shaking, nearly convulsing, and the gun was pointed somewhere in the vicinity of her waistline.

"Sharon, it's all right," I said, and I moved a step toward her.

"No! Get back," she said through her tears. She raised the gun with a trembling hand.

"Please, Sharon," I said in a gentle voice. "There's no point in this. It's too late to bring her back. And Amanda wouldn't want you to kill us. We're not trying to hurt you."

She started to sob again, then sank to her knees and wailed, a mournful, pitiful cry I could hardly bear to hear. I approached her—one small step at a time— and slowly reached for the gun. She let go of it without a struggle.

EPILOGUE

IT's HARD TO DESCRIBE how I feel about Sharon and what she did. There's certainly no question, I obviously can't excuse her killing anyone. In Anna Schulz's case, especially, the motive was pure self-preservation. But with Phillip, it was a little more complicated. When I try to put myself in her place, a mother who'd lost her only child, my heart just aches for her. I really can't imagine anything harder to bear than that. And I think she really convinced herself that Phillip was at fault, even if only to assuage her own guilt for having actually caused the accident. I know it's no excuse, but I still can't help feeling a little sorry for her.

On a lighter note, Brian is still acting weird, though he did take me to Fox & Hounds since I solved the case, and a deal's a deal. He never actually thanked me for my help, but he did say, "Well, you did it again, didn't you?" in a grudging tone of voice. Nice of him. What a guy.

Tom Hanson called to congratulate me and asked me to dinner, but I couldn't make it because I was going out of town. He said he'd call again, but so far, he hasn't.

Emily and Phil took a vacation together for an entire week, and she just called to say they'd be gone for two more days. I can't wait to hear how that turns out.

Sue called and asked me about Gerry and Olivia. I didn't know what to say, and it was clear she already knew, so I just told her the truth. I felt terrible doing it, but I think I'd have felt worse if I'd lied. I didn't make excuses for him but I did tell her I knew he felt bad. I hope they're able to work it out between them. I really like Sue, and for the most part, I like Gerry, too. I think he'd be a lot happier with Sue than with Olivia if he'd just open his eyes. *He* was effusively grateful, by the way, and he asked me to keep in touch.

Peter comes over quite a lot now, more than ever before, and we just sit and talk, and play Monopoly. Even he feels a little sorry for Sharon. He's a good person—very compassionate and perceptive. I can't figure out how that happened. He said Paul's decided to go to law school after all. He was accepted at Marquette and UW but he chose Syracuse because he wanted to get away. A good idea, I think; probably just what he needs.

I introduced my mom to Mrs. Robinson last week. They went shopping together the other day, just the two of them, and then my mother took her to lunch at Watt's Tea Room. I'll have to admit, I was a little jealous, but I think my mom feels a lot better now about our friendship, which makes it all worthwhile, I guess.

I called Nicole Friedman to tell her the news about Phillip and she literally cried with relief. It took me a while to get it out of her, but it turns out she'd suspected Olivia all along. I wonder how Olivia will feel about that.

Margaret Furman sent me some pictures of Scamper and a very kind note. I still miss that little guy, but I really am glad he's with her. At least she's not entirely alone in the world.

Audrey and I go horseback riding every Thursday afternoon now, and we've become pretty good friends. I had her over for dinner the other night and I asked Olivia to join us but she declined. She's still the same snob she always was.

Janice got tears in her eyes when I told her I'd solved the case and Emily actually congratulated me and said she knew all along I'd figure it out. Now isn't *that* amazing? And my mom and dad (who were absolutely furious when they found out what happened) have been bragging about me to the whole neighborhood ever since.

You know, I'll have to admit, I never really believed, after I solved Dave Grezinski's murder, that I'd actually get involved in something like this again. When you do something *once,* that you never would've believed you could do, it feels like a fluke, more luck than anything else. But when you do it *again,* you start to wonder. Maybe I can do this. Maybe I should keep it up. Everyone wants me to quit because they think it's dangerous, which, I suppose, it is in a way. Okay, so it's definitely dangerous, but you have to take risks in life, my father has always told me. When I reminded him of that the other day, he gave me a bewildered look and said this wasn't quite what he had in mind. Well, whether it is or not, I've decided I *am* going to keep it up. Maybe I could get Brian to hire me. What do you think he'd say to that?

Enjoy the mystery and suspense of

POISON APPLES

NANCY MEANS WRIGHT

A VERMONT MYSTERY

"Wright's most gripping and satisfying mystery to date."
—*Female Detective*

"...Wright doesn't put a foot wrong in this well-wrought mystery."
—*Boston Globe*

After tragedy shatters Moira and Stan Earthrowl's lives, running an apple orchard in Vermont gives them a chance to heal. Yet their newfound idyll is short-lived as "accidents" begin to plague the massive orchard: tractor brakes fail, apples are poisoned.

Desperate, Moira turns to neighbor Ruth Willmarth for help. Ruth's investigation reveals a list of possible saboteurs, including a fanatical religious cult and a savvy land developer who, ironically, is Ruth's ex-husband. But deadly warnings make it clear that even Ruth is not immune to the encroaching danger....

If great tales are your motive,
make Worldwide Mystery your partner in crime.
Available September 2001 at your favorite retail outlet.

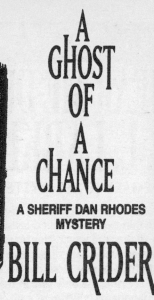

A GHOST OF A CHANCE

**A SHERIFF DAN RHODES
MYSTERY**

BILL CRIDER

Sheriff Dan Rhodes of Blacklin County,
Texas, knows that times may change, but
most things can be explained with a little
common sense—even the "ghost" haunting his jail.
When the body of Ty Berry, the president of one of two
feuding historical societies, is found shot dead in a
freshly dug grave, Rhodes decides the crime is
of a more earthly nature.

The outspoken head of the rival historical society becomes
the second victim, putting Rhodes on the trail of a double
homicide…and of course, one irascible ghost.

Available September 2001 at your favorite retail outlet.

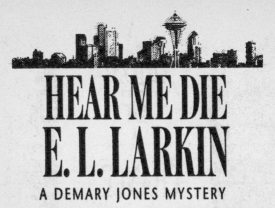

HEAR ME DIE
E. L. LARKIN

A DEMARY JONES MYSTERY

When private investigator Demary Jones gets
a desperate message from friend Sara Garland,
she begins to fear the worst. Her fears are
soon confirmed when Sara disappears. Head
accountant at the highly secretive Electric Toy
Company, Sara isn't the only one in trouble—
the office manager is a victim of a hit-and-run.
Next, the eccentric head of ETC is found
beaten to death.

Though the cops are convinced
Sara is behind the killings,
Demary believes otherwise
and follows a trail of greed
and desperation to a clever
game where toys are
more than child's play.

*Available September 2001
at your favorite retail outlet.*

WELL397

Take 2 books and a surprise gift FREE!

SPECIAL LIMITED-TIME OFFER

Mail to: **The Mystery Library™**
3010 Walden Ave.
P.O. Box 1867
Buffalo, N.Y. 14240-1867

YES! Please send me **2 free books** from the Mystery Library™ and my free surprise gift. Then send me 3 mystery books, first time in paperback, every month. Bill me at the bargain price of $4.69 each plus 25¢ shipping & handling per book and applicable sales tax, if any*. There is no minimum number of books I must purchase. I can always return a shipment at your expense and cancel my subscription. Even if I never buy another book from the Mystery Library™, **the 2 free books and surprise gift are mine to keep forever.**

415 WEN C6PC

Name	(PLEASE PRINT)	
Address		Apt. No.
City	State	Zip

* Terms and prices subject to change without notice. N.Y. residents add applicable sales tax. This offer is limited to one order per household and not valid to present subscribers.

© 1990 Worldwide Library.

MYS01